"You're still angry with me, Roman,"
Manda said. "You're not being reasonable."

His voice was low. "I'm jealous, and jealous men aren't known for being reasonable."

"I don't understand. You're one of the most secure people I've ever met—"

"There are times I'm not at all secure. I can be jealous and possessive and more uncivilized than you can imagine."

"But—"

"You have to know this, because you're one of the things I can't be civilized about." His lips covered hers with so much hard passion that her lungs were robbed of breath and her knees of strength. Heat. She felt a throbbing heat that defied reality. His lips moved to her throat and kissed the cord of her neck. He shuddered, his muscles coiled with tension. "I want to take you, Manda, to crush you and—Tell me to stop. Or I'll hurt you."

His voice was so intense it rocked through her. "I don't want you to stop. But I also don't want you to make love to me in anger. Why would you hurt me?"

"Go away, Manda. I don't want this." His arms tightened around her even as he said the words. "I don't want anyone to have the power to churn me up and turn me inside out. I'll strike out before you get too near. I won't give anyone the power to hurt me—"

She felt tears sting her eyes. "I'll never hurt you, Roman. I only want you to love me. Love me now. . . ."

WHAT ARE *LOVESWEPT* ROMANCES?

They are stories of true romance and touching emotion. We believe those two very important ingredients are constants in our highly sensual and very believable stories in the *LOVESWEPT* line. Our goal is to give you, the reader, stories of consistently high quality that may sometimes make you laugh, sometimes make you cry, but are always fresh and creative and contain many delightful surprises within their pages.

Most romance fans read an enormous number of books. Those they truly love, they keep. Others may be traded with friends and soon forgotten. We hope that each *LOVESWEPT* romance will be a treasure—a "keeper." We will always try to publish

LOVE STORIES YOU'LL NEVER FORGET
BY AUTHORS YOU'LL ALWAYS REMEMBER

The Editors

LOVESWEPT®

Iris Johansen
The Delaneys of Killaroo:
Matilda,
The Adventuress

BANTAM BOOKS
TORONTO • NEW YORK • LONDON • SYDNEY • AUCKLAND

THE DELANEYS OF KILLAROO: MATILDA, THE ADVENTURESS

A Bantam Book / September 1987

ISBN 0-553-21873-5

Published simultaneously in the United States and Canada

Bantam Books are published by Bantam Books, Inc. Its trade-
mark, consisting of the words "Bantam Books" and the por-
trayal of a rooster, is Registered in U.S. Patent and Trademark
Office and in other countries. Marca Registrada. Bantam
Books, Inc., 666 Fifth Avenue, New York, New York 10103.

PRINTED IN THE UNITED STATES OF AMERICA

O   0 9 8 7 6 5 4 3 2 1

For Andrea Cirillo, my agent and friend, who never once let me hear her groan when I told her we were committing this madness again.

And for my good friends, Kay Hooper and Fayrene Preston, who gave me understanding during the good times, support during the bad times, and laughter all the times in between.

About the Delaney Dynasty . . .

When William Delaney was born in 1855, men were men and the West was wild. There were Indian troubles for settlers, but not for the Delaneys; old Shamus had cannily invested one of his sons in a marriage to the daughter of an Apache chief a year or so before young William's birth, which quieted things considerably.

Of course, William, like his uncles before him, gleefully borrowed the Indian custom of counting "coup" and on occasion rode pell-mell though peaceful Apache camps screeching madly and attempting to touch as many braves as possible before they angrily chased him back to Killara, the Delaney homestead.

If he had run true to form, old Shamus, never one to spare the rod, would have punished his grandson severely, but he didn't. He'd learned it was useless in dealing with William. Trees were scarce in southern Arizona, and more than one eastern-made paddle had been worn out on William's unrepentant bottom.

William's father, Desmond, second of Shamus's nine

sons, was killed in the Civil War in 1862, leaving seven-year-old William in the care of his mother, Anne, his grandparents, and various uncles, aunts, and cousins. If he had lived, perhaps Desmond would have controlled his son, for the boy had worshipped him.

Of those left to guard him, only his grandfather had any sort of control over the boy, and that was little enough. Old Shamus, loving his grandchildren as he had his sons, certainly tried. Since William possessed the Delaney charm and was smart enough to turn it to good effect, even Shamus found himself easing up on the boy and remarking that his misdemeanors were products only of high spirits.

The Apaches, understandably annoyed, disagreed; good Irish whiskey was called for then to ease the pain of lacerated tempers.

But as William grew, it began to require more than a friendly drink to repair the consequences of his reckless actions. William rode wild horses, searched far and wide for wild women, and discovered both cards and drink a good ten years before he should have.

At the age of sixteen William had perfected the rather dangerous art of escaping out bedroom windows, enraged husbands and loaded guns one step behind him. He had, with forethought, trained his savage mustang to stand just so beneath those windows, and husbands in jealous pursuit found themselves choking on dust and listening to hearty laughter carried away by fleet hooves.

By the time he was eighteen William had searched out and conquered women within a two-hundred-mile radius of Killara. Indeed, betting in saloons held that a pair of his boots could be found under the bed of every woman under thirty except those William was kin to.

And since old Shamus was no fool, he was well aware of why his grandson often arrived home sketchily attired in only his trousers. Shamus could forgive the womanizing, merely remarking somewhat irritably that he could have raised all nine of his sons and shod them handsomely in the boots William had left behind him.

However, men *were* men then, and the West was still somewhat wild. And, inevitably, William was a bit lazy in leaving a warm bed one night. The jealous husband had burst in prepared, gun in hand and temper raging. William wasted no time with his pants, but grabbed his own gun instead, and when he left that window there was a badly wounded man behind him.

William might have stood his trial; he might even have been acquitted. But he was a gambler, and he knew the odds: at least half the men on any jury would be men he had wronged. So he climbed aboard his bad-tempered mustang and headed west.

He took with him little in the way of material things, confident of his luck, but he did "borrow" a single treasure from the Delaney family coffers. As treasures go, the necklace was worth little. It consisted of three silver medallions, each bearing a turquoise stone. Perhaps William was thinking of his grandfather's lucky number; in any event, he took the necklace.

On the Barbary Coast he found men even more dangerous than those he had left behind him; though there were warm beds aplenty, there were also eager guns and short tempers. William, ever ready to conquer virgin territory, cocked his eye still farther west and boarded a ship.

He wound up, somewhat to his own surprise, in Australia, and liked it enough to remain for a while.

He worked when he had to and gambled when he could, arriving at last on a sheep station—where he hired on happily after a glance at the boss's very pretty daughter.

It was in 1877 when William went to work there, and he lost no time in leaving yet another pair of boots under yet another bed. But William had reckoned without Matthew Devlin, the quiet man whose only child was his daughter, Mary. William went to his wedding as lighthearted as always, unperturbed by the shotgun that had guided his steps to the altar.

William remained for a short time, long enough to tell his bride all about his family in Arizona, about Killara. Truly of Shamus's blood, he wove a splendid story about the relatives half a world away, gifting them with even more wealth and power than what was actually theirs at the time. Then, being William, he cheerfully abandoned his bride and sailed for home, trusting of forgiveness behind him, welcome before him, and having no idea that he had left in Australia something more than a pair of boots and an old necklace.

William found, at Killara, that there was indeed welcome, and that past misdeeds, if not forgotten, were at least viewed as dim and unimportant. He returned to the bosom of his family and never thought to mention the small matter of a wife left behind in Australia's outback.

Unfortunately, none of William's adventures had taught him to curb his recklessness, and he lost no time in reminding people of why he had left Arizona years before. He went his charming way from bad to worse, until even his loving grandfather freely predicted that he would end by getting his neck stretched.

Which, regrettably, is exactly how things turned out.

Mary Delaney was not surprised by William's abandonment; she had loved him and, perhaps remarkably, understood him. She would have as soon attempted to chain the wind as tie William to her side. And she was a strong woman, a proud woman. So she bore her son, Charles, and raised him on the station alone after her father died. She told him often the story of Killara and the Arizona Delaneys, that and a necklace being the only birthright William had left his son.

In his turn, Charles married and fathered a son, passing on the tales of Killara—which was, in reality, by that time, all that William had described and more.

As with many families, the Australian branch of the Delaney clan could boast at least one mystery, and William's son, Charles, was responsible for theirs. At some point in his young life, he attempted to mine gems, and, having barely fathered his own son, he was murdered because of a fabulous gem it was believed he had found. His killers were never caught and the gem, if it existed, vanished.

By the time Spencer Delaney, William's great-grandson, was born in 1935, Killara had become a legend; with news spreading worldwide overnight because of advanced technology, hard facts upheld the legend.

And, pride being a strong Delaney trait, Spencer did not turn to his wealthy American relations when he found himself in financial trouble. Instead, he sold off the larger part of the station to a neighboring station, requiring only that his family be given a two-month option to repurchase the land if it came up for resale.

Killaroo, as the station had been renamed by Mary, was small, and the sale of the land was only temporarily helpful to the family. Spencer, realizing too late what he had given up, worked his fingers to the bone to see his family prosper so the land could be restored to them. As the years passed, it became his obsession. He suffered two minor heart attacks and, ignoring warnings by his doctor that a third would likely kill him, continued to work and scheme to get his land back.

Since Delaneys tended to sire male children, it was somewhat surprising that Spencer had fathered three girls. And though Spencer may well have felt the lack of a son, he loved his girls and wanted the best for them. Sydney, Matilda, and Adelaide, however, wanted their father healthy and free from worry.

And so, when the land once belonging to them came up for sale, the girls resolved to raise the staggering price. They knew, of course, of their American cousins, but none of them even suggested that those strangers be applied to.

Each had a scheme. Each had a talent, or a means to make money quickly. And each was driven, as never before in her life, to attain a very specific goal. They were fighting for their birthright, but, even more, they were fighting for their father's life.

They had two months. Sixty days to do the impossible. And if they knew it *was* impossible, the knowledge was unimportant to them. They were Delaneys, and it was bred into them to know that even the impossible road was traveled one step at a time.

And so they began.

Prologue

Her father was no longer young.

The realization came to Manda with an odd sense of shock. She had never thought Spencer Delaney would grow old. Somehow, he had always been like the land he held so dear—immortal, enduring, and strong enough to turn any defeat into a victory. Yet the man she saw bending over the tractor out in the farmyard was neither strong nor immortal. His hair, which at one time had been brick-red, was now almost entirely gray, and he was thin, too thin. His arm, braced against the seat of the tractor, was not the healthy bronze color she remembered, and it was webbed with a network of prominent blue veins. He shouldn't be out there working, she thought anxiously. They had all tried to stop him, but he had refused to listen. He was in a fever of desperation, and fever victims were seldom reasonable.

"So we're agreed?" Sydney asked.

Manda looked away from the window to Sydney and Addie, who sat across from her at the round oak table. One had to try not to look at him, she told herself. She didn't want to think of her father as old or sick. She always wanted him to be the strong, joyous man she had known as a child. "Right. We've got to keep our individual goals in mind, but if one of us needs help, the other two will come running. We've got to remember this is a joint project. We *all* must succeed."

Addie nodded in agreement. "But what about Dad? It's important we keep this a secret. There's potential danger in all our plans, and we can't worry him." She made a face. "You two have it a heck of a lot easier than I do. He's bound to hear about what I'm doing."

She was right. The newspaper stories that were sure to come would give Addie a king-size headache. Manda felt a throb of sympathy as she realized how much Addie was going to hate being the focus of attention of the entire country.

"Do the best you can," Sydney said. "And if you need any help, ring us."

On the surface Sydney appeared as coolly controlled as ever, but the tension she was experiencing could be seen in her slim, graceful hands that were folded tightly on the table. Manda felt a momentary spurt of exasperation mixed with affection. Sydney was playing the older sister again by trying to keep them all calm.

"I'll be on the move constantly, so I'll check in often," Addie said. "And since I'll be closest to home, I'll be the one to keep an eye on Dad."

"Good," Sydney said. "Be sure and let us know if anything changes with him."

Suddenly Manda's exasperation at her sister disappeared like morning mist in the sunlight. She wanted to jump up and run around the table to give her older sister a big hug. It wouldn't take much effort to break through Sydney's fragile, brittle facade to uncover the loving woman beneath. She responded to affection like a thirsty blossom to spring rain. Manda heaved a sigh and decided she'd better leave well enough alone. Sydney needed the crystal wall she had built around her emotions. She drew a deep, shaky breath. "Lord, I'm scared. What if we blow it?"

Addie and Sydney looked at her in surprise. For Pete's sake, Manda thought, didn't they think she ever worried or became frightened or uncertain? It was true she was prone to act first and think later, but this was different.

The Black Flame. The forty-five-carat black opal was the stuff of which fables were made. Who knew if it even existed? It might be only a legend passed down through the family for generations. Charles Delaney might have been boasting when he had written to his wife, Mignon, that he had uncovered and then hidden a giant opal from the human predators who roamed Deadman's Ridge. And, if he had found it, why did she believe she could discover its hiding place, when, after eighty years, the jewel had never been found?

"I'm scared too," Addie said softly.

Manda smiled gratefully at Addie. Somehow she doubted Addie was truly frightened; it was likely she was trying to make her feel better by placing herself in the same boat as Manda. Addie's gaze was filled with pure determination.

"We all are," Sydney said. She reached out and tightly clasped hands with her sisters. "But we won't fail, because we can't." She smiled with an effort.

"This isn't another one of Manda's trips to the sea. This dream has got to become a reality."

Manda felt her heart lift. What was she worried about? Together, she, Addie, and Sydney were an unbeatable combination. They had only to set out on their separate courses, steering full speed ahead. The navigational metaphor made her smile. In spite of Sydney's denigrating reference to her trip to the sea, that particular journey hadn't been a total failure. She had always believed that if they hadn't been discovered, they would have made it all the way.

Well, now they had another chance, another odyssey to make together, and this time there would be no stopping them.

One

"It's no use, Jacto." Manda jerked a blue and white handkerchief from the back pocket of her cut-off jeans and used it to wipe the perspiration from her forehead. "There's no place down in the primary tunnel where old Charlie could have hidden his cache. I've looked everywhere, and I've seen only dust, rusted machinery, and rubble."

Jacto handed her a cup of tea. His hollow-cheeked black face was as impassive as always. "So you will try another tunnel tomorrow," he said calmly. "You said there were four more tunnels in the mine. You will find the treasure eventually."

Manda sank down onto the ground in front of the campfire, crossing her legs and cradling the tin cup between her palms. "But will it be in time? I spent three days searching that blasted tunnel and didn't come up with a clue as to where Charlie could have hidden the jewel. And this was the shortest tunnel in the mine." She sighed as her despondent gaze traveled over the desolate terrain. The vast opal field that stretched in every direction was pockmarked with nearly a hundred mine openings that reminded her of the craters of the moon. "We're lucky everyone believes the field is played out, or we'd really be in trouble. Can you imagine me marching up to a miner who had filed on Charlie's old claim to ask him if I could please search his mine?" She made a face. "He'd probably blow me away. In Coober Pedy the miners protect their claims with Doberman pinschers and shotguns."

Jacto waited. Manda Delaney wasn't often discouraged, and he knew this mood wouldn't last long. He had only to be silent, and her usual sunny optimism would reassert itself.

She took a sip of tea. "Well, I still have four weeks, and that can be a long time."

"You are obviously trying to stretch it longer," Jacto said dryly. "You have not slept more than a few hours a night for the past three days."

"I don't need a lot of sleep. Four hours is usually enough for me. It's too hot to sleep anyway."

Jacto nodded. "Over a hundred degrees. It must be ten degrees hotter down in the mine."

"At least." Manda lifted her shoulder-length hair and wiped her neck. No breeze blew to cool the hot night, but the air still felt good. She should have braided her hair after she had washed it earlier that afternoon, she realized, but it had felt so good to leave it flowing free after having confined it for the last few days. She had felt stifled and confined herself in the mine, and being out in the open was inexpressibly soothing. How beautiful the tranquil desert night was, with its limitless space and blazing stars. "And sometimes the dust is so thick I can hardly breathe."

Jacto's lids veiled his eyes. "You could give up.

After all, you are only a woman. No one expects you to undergo such discomfort."

Manda lifted her head like a racehorse who had just heard the bell at the starting gate. "What do you mean, only a—" She stopped and began to chuckle. "Lord, I must be more tired than I thought. I almost rose to the bait. You're a wicked old man, Jacto." She took another sip of tea. "And I'm a fool to get upset when I've scarcely begun to search. Right?"

The faintest trace of a smile deepened the corners of the Aborigine's lips. "I do not presume to judge."

Manda slowly shook her head, her amber eyes once more snapping with their customary good humor and vitality. "Not verbally anyway. You just sit there behind that inscrutable mask, and let me talk myself in doing exactly what you want me to do."

"What *you* want to do," he corrected her mildly. "Your treasure has no value to me. However, I find it interesting to watch you search. You are usually not this . . . intense."

He realized at once he had used the wrong word. Manda was always intense about everything she did, every project she undertook. Yet her intensity always held an element of joyousness, as if the journey itself were as thrilling as reaching the final destination. But, the joyousness she usually felt was missing during this particular quest. Manda, despite her wanderlust, was very close to her family, and he should have known she would not take her father's plight lightly. No, the word he should have chosen was *desperate*.

"I'm frightened," she said with childlike simplicity. "Nothing has ever meant this much to me before. Dad has always given me whatever I needed —love, security, understanding. Everything. He's never really needed anything from me, and now that he does need something, I'm scared to death I won't be able to give it to him." She shook her head. "I guess I have trouble understanding people who think their world will stop spinning if they lose a piece of land, a house, a particular possession that's important to them. People are important, but things . . . I just can't understand it. There are so many beautiful places to see, so many wonderful roads to travel, why kill yourself trying to hold on to possessions? Who knows? Maybe what you'll find ahead is better than what you have at the moment."

"Your father does not think as you do."

"No." She drew up her knees, rested her chin on them, and gazed thoughtfully at the flickering flames of the campfire. "He loves every inch of Killaroo. It nearly destroyed him when he lost that land." She was silent a moment. "He wasn't always so devoted to the land, you know. Before he married my mother, he traveled all over Australia from Tasmania to Queensland to Western Australia. He used to tell me such wonderful stories about his travels when I was a little girl." A tiny frown knotted her brow. "He . . . changed."

"People do change."

"Why?" she whispered. "He was so happy. You should have seen his face when he was telling me about rafting down the Murray River. He was blazing with happiness. Do you know what I mean?"

Jacto knew very well what she meant. He had seen the same blaze burning bright within Manda on many occasions. "Yes."

"I don't change. You don't either, Jacto. I don't understand why other people do."

"Perhaps someday you will understand."

"I don't know if I want to. I don't want to be driven like my father. I don't want to be caught in the trap of caring about possessions." She shifted her shoulders as if a burden weighed upon them. "I want to enjoy life." A sudden smile lit her thin face with warmth. "We do enjoy life, don't we, Jacto?"

"Yes."

"You're about as communicative as a baobab tree tonight."

"How do you know a baobab can't communicate? It is a spirit tree. Perhaps you haven't listened to its message."

"Is that statement supposed to have some hidden meaning? I'm too tired to decipher your cryptic little puzzles tonight, Jacto." She smothered a yawn. "I think I'll try to sleep a little before dawn. I'm not looking forward to doing the preliminary exploration on the next tunnel, and there's some lumber blocking the entrance that will have to be removed."

"I will do it while you sleep."

She shook her head. "Wait for me. It's too much for one person to do alone. You do too much for me as it is. When I asked you to come along, it was for your company, not for your strong back. This is my job." The firelight danced in the golden waves of her thick and vibrant hair. "Even if I am 'only' a woman, I believe I can handle it by myself."

"I will think about what you have said."

"Now, don't give me one of your noncommittal answers. I know damn well you mean you'll think about what I said and then go ahead and do whatever you want to do anyway. I want your word you won't—" She broke off. "What on earth is that?"

Jacto looked over his shoulder to follow her gaze

from the ridge on which they were sitting to the horizon. "Lights," he said matter-of-factly.

"I know they're lights," she said impatiently. "I have eyes." She set down her cup and jumped to her feet, watching the thick veil of dust which was rising into the sky. "Good heavens, it looks like a caravan. There must be at least a dozen cars and trucks coming this way. What could they be doing out here in the desert in the middle of the night?"

"The fact that it's the middle of the night means nothing. Most work and travel is done at night to avoid the heat. You know that, Manda." Yet it was like Manda to have conveniently forgotten that information; it would have detracted from the intriguing possibilities she saw coming toward her. "We will find out soon enough. The road leads only to Deadman's Ridge."

"Oh, Jacto, how can you be so calm?"

"Oh, Manda, how can you be so excited?"

"I'm going down to meet them." She was already running toward the road, which was several hundred yards away.

"Be carefu—" He stopped. It would be of no use to caution her. She wouldn't listen. Something new and different was on the horizon and Manda was running to meet it.

Jacto reached over and picked up his hunting knife from beneath his bedroll. He stood up with an effortless flowing motion and sauntered after the swiftly flying figure of Manda Delaney.

"Good Lord, why on earth did you decide to come out here to the back of beyond?" Brent Penrose slowly shook his head as he gazed gloomily at the flat brown desolate land around him. The ancient desert was stark, bare of vegetation except for an occasional bearding of wheat-colored spinifex scrub. "I'm warning you, Roman, I have a clause in my contract that holds you liable if we fall off the edge of the world."

Roman Gallagher's lips twitched as he glanced at the man sitting beside him in the open Jeep. "Now I wonder why my lawyers didn't bring that clause to my attention."

"Small print." Brent coughed. "There's another clause regarding dust asphyxiation. You should have passed out gas masks before you started this safari into hell."

"I'll remember to do that next time," Roman assured him solemnly. "I forgot how fragile the Homo Hollywoodantes could be. Now, let me see, in your last picture you clawed your way up the wall of a cliff, swung from the yardarm of a schooner, and—"

"You mean my double did. Do you think I'd risk my valuable neck on stuff like that?"

"Yes." Roman's dark eyes narrowed with sudden shrewdness. "You perform all your own stunts. You also do summer stock for which you are paid peanuts, so that you can take a stab at acting in Eugene O'Neill's and Tennessee Williams's plays. Don't try to feed me your phony Hollywood image. When you came to me and asked for this part, I made damn sure I knew exactly who and what you were. I always look a gift horse in the mouth."

Brent pursed his lips in a soundless whistle. "I've heard you did, but I wasn't aware you were quite so thorough." He had heard a hell of a lot more about Roman Gallagher. He was said to be a workaholic who expected his team to follow his example or drop by the wayside. He was supremely cynical and could be obstinate as the devil. He also had a passionate hatred for the paparazzi and was the despair of his studio's publicity department. On the plus side, he was brilliant, perhaps the best director since John Huston, absolutely professional, and capable of drawing Academy Award-winning performances from even the most mundane actors. "Sorry. My line of bull has become so ingrained, it has a habit of tumbling out automatically." He suddenly sounded weary. "Sometimes I myself forget what's real and what the press has cooked up."

Roman smiled grimly. "Well, you won't have to worry about newspaper reporters at Deadman's Ridge. I don't allow reporters on any of my locations."

"Deadman's Ridge." Brent savored the words with obvious enjoyment. "It does have a certain ring to it, but it sounds more like a setting for a horror film than for a historical drama."

"At the turn of the century this area had its share of horror stories. Only the opal field at Lightning Ridge had a history of more violence. Greed, murder, and a struggle against the elements—who could ask for better ingredients for a major motion picture?"

"Going fishing for another Academy Award?" Brent asked, grinning. "I hope to hell you catch the big one because I'm going to be right behind you with a net to gather anything you might want to throw back."

"I'll let you worry about the awards," Roman said. "I have enough to do just trying to make a decent film." Having his film *Fulfillment* win the Best Picture award the previous year had stunned Roman, but he didn't fool himself into believing the award meant the picture was any better than the one he'd done the year before. Studio politics and public sentiment could make all the difference in a film's success or failure. He'd learned a long time ago it was safer to put a personal sense of creative achievement before the accolades of his peers. "*The Ridge* is going to be a damn fine film, Brent. Count on it."

"I am," Brent said soberly. Then a roguish smile lit his face. "Even to the point of giving up wine, women, and song." He shifted in his seat. "My hind quarters are getting numb. How close are we to this haven of inspiration you've chosen as our home away from home? Didn't anyone ever tell you a star is entitled to a Rolls-Royce limo, not a Jeep with no damn shock absorbers?"

"We're climbing Deadman's Ridge right now. When we scouted this location, we found a place to set up the trailers and equipment on the east ridge. The opal field itself should be around the next turn."

"I can hardly wait. I've always wanted to see a deserted opal field at three o'clock in the—"

"What the hell! There's a woman standing in the middle of the road!" Roman's foot stomped on the brakes of the Jeep. The vehicle swerved and then skidded to the side of the road. He could hear the screech of brakes from the long column of trucks and trailers he was leading. The sound was immediately followed by the blistering curses of the drivers.

"Well, there goes tomorrow's shooting." Brent gingerly touched the bruise he'd just acquired on his forehead from banging his head on the dashboard of the Jeep. "Unless you'd care to write in a barroom brawl. I'm going to have a devil of a bruise on my matchless profile."

"I told you to wear your seat belt." Roman's tone

was impatient as he unbuckled his own belt and stepped out of the Jeep.

"Who would have expected an accident in the middle of the desert?" Brent asked plaintively. "You were surprised too."

"Are you all right?"

The breathless question came from the woman who had run up to the Jeep as soon as it had come to a halt. Her cinnamon-colored hair shimmered in the headlights, sparkling as though touched by a golden hand. Roman was fascinated for a fleeting instant by that brilliant halo of color. He shifted his gaze to her face. "What the hell did you think you were doing? I almost ran over you."

"Lord, I'm sorry. I didn't realize you were going so fast. I just wanted to . . ." Her eyes widened in amazement. "You're Roman Gallagher. How wonderful. I've always wanted to meet you."

"Yes." Hell, not another would-be starlet he thought. He'd had his fill of actresses throwing themselves into his path in the hope of getting a part in one of his films. His lips curved in involuntary amusement at the aptness of the thought. This particular woman, he had to admit, was more enterprising than most. Not everyone would go to the bother of throwing herself in front of his Jeep to feign an accidental meeting in the middle of the desert. She had obviously planned her little charade down to the last detail. Her cut-off jeans were sun-faded and a little soiled, and her white tennis shoes were scuffed and dusty. Her sleeveless, low-necked white T-shirt was dampened in places by perspiration and clung to her full breasts. His gaze also clung to her breasts, and he was startled to feel a hot ache in his loins. It didn't make a damn bit of sense to him. She wasn't even sexy. Yet his reaction had been unmistakable. A tingle of annoyance went through him.

She smiled, and he inhaled sharply. Warmth. Lord, her smile illuminated her thin face like the Southern Cross illuminated the night sky.

"I love your films," she said. "I thought *Fulfillment* was terrific, and I've seen all your documentaries. My favorite was the one you did on the Barrier Reef."

He tried to mask his surprise. She had clearly done her homework. He hadn't done a documentary in seven years, and at that time his audience had been extremely small. "Thank you. I enjoyed filming it, even though the subject of the reef had been done a hundred or so times before."

"But not like you did it. The underwater scenes were . . ." She took an eager step closer, her amber eyes shining in the reflected beam of the headlights. She met his gaze and suddenly her eyes widened in curious surprise, and she forgot what she wanted to say. Then she shook her head as if to clear it and laughed uncertainly. "There aren't any words to describe that film. I wanted to hop on the next boat to the reef."

"I'm surprised you didn't."

She whirled to her left, and faced the man who had just stepped down from the truck directly behind the Jeep. She squinted into the shadows as she tried to match a face with the familiar voice. "Dennis?" Then, as the man came into the perimeter of the headlights, his gray-flecked sandy brown hair and rough-hewn features became clearer. She flew across the road and into his arms, and gave him an enthusiastic hug. "Dennis Billett, what on earth are you doing here?"

"I could ask you the same thing." His hazel eyes

were twinkling down at her. "Except I've given up being surprised at the places you turn up. Nowadays I just accept the fact that if there's excitement or trouble or danger around, sooner or later you'll be there."

"I hate to interrupt this reunion, but I have a location to set up." Roman's tone was caustic. For some irrational reason he was displeased at the sight of her in Billet's arms. "You know this woman, Dennis?"

Dennis nodded. "We go back a long way." He placed his arm companionably around her waist as he turned to face Roman. "Manda Delaney, this is my boss, Roman Gallagher."

Manda was frowning. "Location? You're going to set up a movie location here? But you can't do that!"

"I have a drawerful of permits back in Sydney that says the opposite." Roman's lips tightened. "I'd better damn well be able to do it. Are you saying you have a prior claim?"

"No, not exactly." She ran her fingers through her shining hair. "I tried to get one, but the authorities said the entire area had already been leased. I thought it was a mistake. No one comes to Deadman's Ridge anymore. There haven't been any opals found in this field for over twenty-five years."

"Which is why I had no trouble obtaining a three-month lease on the ridge."

"You're going to be here for three months?" The dismay on her face was unmistakable. "Look, can't you go somewhere else? I know I don't have a legal permit, but I was here first, and my business is very important."

He was staring at her in disbelief. "Do you realize

how much money I'd lose per day looking for another location?"

She made a face. "No chance?"

"No chance." His eyes narrowed. "May I assume you're not an actress then?"

"Me?" She was astonished. "Why would you think I was an actress?"

He stiffened. "What's your business here? Are you a newspaper reporter?"

"What is this? Twenty Questions?"

His lips twisted. "I know you people consider questions the perogative of the press, but you should have thought of that before you decided to trespass on my land. Lord, I thought I'd gotten away from vultures like you."

"I'm *not* a reporter."

"Then just what is your business here, Miss Delaney?"

"Manda." She smiled and again he felt warmth radiate through him. "I'm afraid my business is of a private nature. However, I assure you it's most urgent. I promise I won't get in your way if you let me stay." Her voice dropped to wheedling softness. "I know you'll understand."

Dennis Billet suddenly burst into laughter. "Manda, you never change. Be careful, Roman, she'll be talking you out of your mobile home in another minute."

She had come very close to getting what she wanted from him. Roman felt a flare of anger when he realized that if he hadn't been jarred by Dennis's obvious amusement, she would probably have done so. "I can't help you. I've made it a rule to close my set to outsiders." Roman got back into the Jeep and started the ignition. He noticed Dennis's arm still held the woman in a casual embrace, and he found his pilot's familiarity with Manda Delaney oddly annoying. The woman was obviously an accomplished charmer and accustomed to getting her own way with men. Well, she would find he distinctly disliked being used by anyone, women in particular. "I'll give you one day to pack up and get off the property."

"But you don't understand. I can't—" The rest of her sentence was lost as the Jeep roared to life. "I *have* to stay here. There are reasons . . ."

The Jeep jumped forward as he pressed the accelerator. A few seconds later he'd driven several yards down the road.

"You weren't very polite," Brent drawled. "You didn't introduce me, and I got the distinct impression that something about the lady annoyed the hell out of you. Pity. She could have been very entertaining to have around. You could have thought about *my* convenience, Roman. You drag me out here in the wilds with an all-male cast, forbid me to seduce any of the women on your production crew, and then send packing the only alluring woman who crosses our path. How inconsiderate can you be?"

"I'm sure you'll survive. Besides, she wasn't all that pretty."

"You don't think so? Personally, I prefer the unconventional type."

"Too thin."

"But magnificent breasts."

Roman didn't want to think about her full breasts pressed against the thin white cotton of her T-shirt. The memory aroused the same physical response he had experienced when he had looked at her a few moments before. Damn! What the hell was wrong with him? He was scarcely sex-starved. The night before he had been provided with innovative erotic entertainment by a call girl who had enjoyed her work as much as he had enjoyed it. She had used him, but at least she had been honest about it. He could tolerate a mutually gratifying exchange of favors. In fact, he preferred it to the hypocrisy to which he'd been subjected during the past few years. He knew he was no Adonis. What he couldn't stand was a woman who tried to manipulate him into doing what she wanted by using sex as a weapon. Manda Delaney was obviously a woman who was skilled in the use of that particular weapon. At last he said, "I didn't notice her figure."

Brent glanced sidewise at him, and then smiled. "Oh, yes, you noticed all right. Is it okay if I go after her and offer her my sympathy, my magnificent body, and anything else she'll accept?"

"Why should I care? She's nothing to me." Roman's hands tightened unconsciously on the steering wheel. "Though I don't think it's worth your while. She'll be gone tomorrow, and that doesn't give you much time to lure her into your bed."

"Long enough. Haven't you heard I'm irresistible? All my press clippings say so." The amusement was abruptly gone from Brent's expression. "If you want her yourself, I'll back off, Roman. My role in your film means too much to me to jeopardize our professional relationship over a woman."

For the briefest instant Roman was tempted to tell him to back off, to keep away from her. The instinct was as brutally primitive as the hardening between his thighs. Lord, what had gotten into him tonight? There was no way he was going to involve himself with Manda Delaney even to obtain a temporary sexual release. Her appearance in his life had been entirely too coincidental, and her reluctance to tell him the purpose of her business in the opal field was distinctly suspicious. She could be anything from a hooker on the make, to one of the paparazzi out to get an exclusive interview. He forced himself to relax, and his moment of insanity passed. He shrugged. "Do what you like. She doesn't appeal to me. I've never cared for women with that color hair."

"Oh, dear!" Manda was disappointed as she gazed at the Jeep moving swiftly up the track. "He's going to be very difficult. I really didn't need this. Not now."

"I don't suppose you'd care to tell me why you're out here in the middle of the desert?" Dennis drew her to the side of the road as the caravan of trucks began to rumble after the Jeep. "You're not prospecting by any chance?"

"No." She changed the subject. "What are you doing in a truck, for heaven's sake. Where's your Cessna?"

"The engine needed an overhaul. They're going to test-fly it out here to the location in a few days."

"You're still a professional pilot?" She held up her hand to stop him from answering. "Of course you are. What a stupid question. I know you'd never give it up. How long have you worked for Roman Gallagher?"

"Nine months this time. I was also his private pilot several years ago when he was making documentaries, but he's been back in Australia for only a little over a year." His eyes narrowed on her face. "I don't know what you want from him, but I'd advise you to be very careful, Manda, my love. Gallagher has been the target of every starlet in Australia and the United States since he won the award for directing *Fulfillment*. He's a hell of a lot more cynical now than when I knew him in the old days."

Dennis's assessment was no surprise to Manda. Cynicism was imprinted on Roman Gallagher's face for anyone to see. It was visible in the lines grooving his lean cheeks and the glittering darkness of his eyes. She had found herself staring at the filmmaker in helpless fascination, watching his expressions change, listening to the deep timbre of his voice. Something crazy and totally unexpected had happened. She had never felt an instant emotional leap of response and empathy toward a man before. It couldn't happen so quickly, could it? She had always laughed at the idea of love at first sight. Sexual attraction at first sight she could believe with no problems, but love?

It couldn't be love. The feelings of tenderness she was experiencing had to be an illusion brought upon her by weariness and lack of sleep. The man had been rude, bitter, and unrelenting. The next time she saw him she would probably realize how idiotic she was being. Still . . . "I need some information, Dennis. Will you help me?"

"Why not? You always did manage to make things interesting. I think I'd like to keep you around for a while."

"Tell me about Roman Gallagher. Is he married?"

"No."

"Women?"

"He's no celibate, but he didn't bring a woman with him from Sydney. He doesn't allow anyone or anything to interfere when he's working." He studied her curiously. "Do I detect a personal note of interest?"

"Maybe. I'll let you know later when I sort out my emotions. Right now I feel as if I've been struck by lightning."

He gave a long, low whistle. "I think this job may

prove a tad more intriguing than the usual. As I remember, you were always the Sheila dealing the lightning." He grinned. "I guess I should have expected the unexpected from you. Tell me, did you happen to notice the other man in the Jeep?"

"No." She hadn't been able to take her eyes from Roman Gallagher. He had seemed to occupy the entire horizon. "Was he someone special?"

"Several million of his fans think so, and I'm sure they'd be most insulted that you didn't think him important enough to deserve your attention. He's Brent Penrose, the American movie star."

"That's nice," she said vaguely. She touched her hair. "Does he like women with this color hair?"

"Penrose?"

"Of course not. Roman Gallagher."

"I have no idea. I've seen him only with brunettes."

"Rats."

"You're really serious about this," he said thoughtfully. "I never would have believed it in a hundred years. You ignore America's heartthrob and lose your head over Gallagher. He's not even what you would call a pleasant-looking bloke."

"No, he isn't." When she had first caught sight of him, she had thought him quite unattractive. None of his features seemed to go together. His long nose and heavy-lidded eyes were a little Oriental-looking, and his lips were a firm, hard line. His left cheek was marred by a jagged white scar that zagged from his temple to the corner of his mouth. She supposed his most attractive feature were his marvelously expressive dark eyes. No, that wasn't true. His sable-black hair was really quite beautiful, thick, lustrous, and wavy. She wished she could remember other physical details about him. She guessed he was at least six foot five, but she had been too absorbed by the sheer impact of the man to notice anything else in detail. "I wouldn't believe it either." She sighed. "And it's the wrong time, dammit. I don't want this. It's crazy. Maybe it's just a temporary infatuation that will go away as quickly as it came. Lord, I hope so."

"What if it doesn't?"

She turned to look at him in surprise. "Well, then I'll just have to make him care for me too. What else can I do?"

Dennis chuckled and gave her an affectionate hug. "What else?" he repeated. "You're the most honest woman I've ever known, Manda. I'd forgotten how direct and single-minded you can be. If you want something, you just go after it."

Troubled, she frowned. "You make me sound like a heartless bitch. Am I really like that, Dennis?"

His palm reached up to caress her cheek. No, there was nothing heartless about Manda. She was impulsive and headstrong, but there was no lack of caring in her emotional makeup. He had sometimes thought she would be better off if she didn't care quite so much. She would give away anything she owned without thinking twice. It was ridiculously easy to prey on Manda's sympathies. He had done it quite shamelessly himself on a number of occasions. "You're not so bad, mate," he said gruffly. "At least you manage to keep a man amused."

She wrinkled her nose at him. "Thanks a heap. I'll know better than to come to you for any testimonials." She stepped back. "Come on over and say hello to Jacto."

"He's still with you?" Dennis's brows rose in surprise.

"We couldn't get along without each other. We're

two of a kind. No one else understands . . ." She trailed off as she turned away. "He'll be glad to see you. I think he always liked you, Dennis."

"Did he? I'm glad to hear it. I sure couldn't tell. Jacto isn't exactly talkative."

Manda laughed and the silvery sound floated back to Dennis as she preceded him across the road toward the place where Jacto sat waiting with his legs crossed like a serene Buddha. "Jacto may not talk much," she said, "but he always manages to make himself understood."

Dennis could second that statement. The old Aborigine could express more mocking amusement with his blank stare than anyone he had ever met. Somehow Jacto had always made Dennis a little uneasy. Those glowing dark eyes of his seemed to see entirely too much. As far as he could tell in the moonlit darkness, Jacto had changed very little since he had last seen him. The old man's cropped hair was still a grizzled gray, and his worn dark trousers and checked shirt hung loosely on his tall wiry body. Dennis couldn't make out the expression on Jacto's thin face, but he'd bet his Cessna that it contained the same mockery he remembered.

Manda stopped in the middle of the road, her gaze on the caravan which had left the road and was bumping over the rough ground on the eastern perimeter of the opal field. Some of the trucks had already stopped and she could see people jumping out of the vehicles and starting to set up the camp.

The desert was no longer tranquil, and her entire situation was now fraught with complications. Yet, as she stood there looking at the energetic bustling of the production crew, she felt a familiar shiver of excitement.

Change. Things were changing, events were going to occur, people would act and react. How she loved adventure and change, and this time it had the potential to be more exciting than ever before. Because Roman Gallagher was somewhere in that crowd of men and machinery, and, perhaps, he might be the greatest adventure of all.

"Manda?" Dennis was standing beside her. "Is something wrong?"

She shook her head and her cinnamon-gold hair shimmered in the moonlight. "I don't think so." She started toward Jacto again. "I think it's possible that everything might be very right indeed."

Two

Manda took a deep breath, squared her shoulders, and then knocked firmly on the metal door of the small mobile home.

"Roman's not there. I think he went out to scout locations with the assistant director. Will I do?"

She turned to face the man who was strolling toward her from the direction of another mobile home a few yards away. His handsome features were familiar. Brent Penrose. She would have recognized him at once last night except his modishly cut golden hair had seemed darker in the moonlight.

She smiled. "Not unless you can give me permission to stay here at Deadman's Ridge. Do you have any influence with Mr. Gallagher?"

"Not much." He leaned lazily back against the metal door of the mobile home with his thumbs hooked in the front pockets of his jeans, and studied her. "You clean up quite nicely. Not that you weren't appetizing enough before." His glance wandered slowly down her body to her long, tanned legs, which were shown off to advantage by her khaki shorts. "I almost wish I could claim to be able to sway Roman. Would it help my case if I told you how rich and famous I am?"

"Your case?"

"Bed."

She laughed with genuine amusement. "You're very blunt. No, I'm afraid it wouldn't help. I don't make sexual bargains."

"Well, I thought it was worth a try. No offense?"

"No offense." It would have been difficult for her to take offense at Brent Penrose. There was something very appealing about his smile and she appreciated the honesty of his approach. "I suppose I should be flattered. You must have your pick of bedmates."

"Not out here in the wilds," he said with engaging frankness. "There's no one to impress on Deadman's Ridge but the dingos. It's going to be a long stretch of celibacy." He arched a brow inquiringly. "Unless you'd care to change your mind?"

She shook her head as a smile tugged at her lips. "I believe you'll survive. Why did you come out here if you felt that way?"

"Because Roman is giving me the chance to prove I'm not just a pretty face." His smile faded. "I hit it big in a couple of adventure films that were block-busters, and now the powers that be in Hollywood have me typecast. I can *act*, dammit, but no one will give me the chance to prove it."

"I'm sure you can act," she said quietly. "I've never seen one of your films, but I know Mr. Gallagher's work. I don't think he'd entrust the lead in one of his movies to someone he couldn't count on for a top performance."

"No?" For an instant there was a shadow of uncertainty on Brent's face before he smiled. "You can see I have my moments of insecurity. You're very good for my ego, Manda. A woman who doesn't want my money, my body, or the cachet of saying she slept with Brent Penrose, and yet is still willing to offer faith and encouragement. Perhaps I'd better try to keep you around to bolster my sagging confidence in times of need."

She grinned back at him. "I'll be glad to enlist all the help I can get. I don't think I impressed your Mr. Gallagher much last night."

"I wouldn't say that. I had the distinct feeling he was very impressed." A curious smile touched his lips. "Some men aren't as uncomplicated as yours truly. Roman can be very . . . stubborn."

She made a face. "Darn it, I didn't want to hear that. Oh, well, I can be pretty determined myself when it comes to locking horns."

He reached out and gently tucked a shining strand of hair back from her temple. "I'm not about to endanger my part in this picture, but outside of that, I'll help all I can. Deal?"

"Deal," she agreed softly.

"If you're through making your 'arrangements,' Brent, I'd appreciate it if you'd move your butt and let me into my trailer." Roman's tone was filled with sarcasm. They both turned to look at him in surprise as he appeared at their side. He was dressed in tight moleskin trousers in a pale shade of beige, brown suede desert boots, and a khaki bush shirt. He looked warm, exasperated, and definitely on edge. "I've been wandering around for the last four hours in this damn hundred-degree heat setting up my story board, and I need a cold shower and a long drink."

He glanced at Manda and she felt a little shock at the cold ferocity she saw in his face. The man obviously had a savage temper, and a good deal of his fierceness was being aimed at her. "Since you came to an 'agreement' with our little trespasser, why don't you take her along to your own trailer?"

"I'd be delighted, but the lady has business with you." Brent's bright blue eyes were suddenly glinting with mischief as he added, "First." He turned away. "Just knock on the door when you're through, Manda. I'll be waiting." His tone was intimately husky. "Very impatiently."

Manda gave him an exasperated glance. It appeared Brent had a puckish sense of humor, but she wished he hadn't chosen to display it at this particular moment. Roman Gallagher was in a bad enough mood already. "He's right. I have to talk to you. I won't keep you long."

"I'm sure you won't." Roman's lips twisted as he opened the heavy metal door. "We mustn't keep Brent waiting." He motioned for her to precede him into the mobile home. "After you. We should be able to get this over fairly quickly."

He meant it would take very little time to say no, Manda thought ruefully. Well, he was going to be surprised.

The mobile home was more spacious than it appeared to be from outside and was composed of a small kitchenette, a living room, and, to her left, a door which presumably led to the bath and sleeping quarters.

He gestured to a beige- and tangerine-flowered couch across the room. "Sit down. Drink?"

"No, thank you."

He shut the door and suddenly she felt uneasy.

The confines of the room made her acutely conscious of Roman's virile physical presence. Her gaze clung in fascination to the slide of muscles of his long back, outlined beneath his khaki shirt. As he walked toward the refrigerator, he exhibited a loose-limbed grace that reminded her of the way Jacto moved, but the resemblance ended there. Gallagher was neither thin nor wiry. The powerful muscles of his thighs and calves were clearly distinguished by the moleskin trousers he wore. She found herself wondering how those muscles would feel beneath her palms. Would they be smooth or heavily corded . . .

"You don't mind if I do?"

Her gaze flew up to meet his, and hot color rushed to redden her cheeks. "What?"

He didn't speak for a moment, his expression as startled as her own. Manda could feel the air between them thicken with electricity. The bottle of cola in his hand stopped in mid-motion over a tall glass. His gaze was intent as it moved over her.

She could feel it as if it were a touch, brushing the tips of her breasts that thrust against the thin knit of her yellow T-shirt, and then moving down past her taut stomach to her legs. This was the second time in a matter of minutes, she realized, that her body had been appraised by a man, but her present reaction was wildly different from the amusement she had experienced when Brent had looked her over.

She could almost feel Roman's long, tanned fingers rubbing the soft insides of her thighs. Her lips parted to permit more oxygen to enter her lungs. She must be insane, she told herself. She had experienced sexual arousal before, but never anything as intense as what she felt now. The palms of her hands were tingling. There was a pulsating throb between her thighs that was beginning to spread throughout her body, even to the sensitive arches of her feet.

His gaze finally left her, and he looked down at the cola he'd poured into the glass. "I asked you if you minded if I had a drink?" he muttered. "I think."

"Oh, no, of course not," she said quickly. She searched desperately for something, anything, to say that would cut the electricity flowing between them. "This is a very nice mobile home. They're really amazingly efficient, aren't they? I lived in one for three months in Arnhem Land and was more comfortable than I would have believed possible. Of course, I'd just come back from a rough trek through the Blue Mountains, so any home would have seemed luxurious by comparison."

"You move around a lot, don't you?" He leaned his elbow on the beige ceramic tile surface of the bar. "No wonder you and Dennis are chums. He doesn't like to stay in one place either."

"You're not exactly a homebody yourself. You've made documentaries all over the world, and Dennis said you've just come back from Hollywood."

His brows rose as he took a sip of cola. "You're very well informed. Traveling is part of my job."

"Mine too." She shrugged. "Well, that's not quite true. I'm working toward a degree in geology and some of my travels have been connected with my studies, but not all of them. I guess I just like to go walkabout, like Jacto. There's so much to do and so much to see . . ." She trailed off. "I suppose you think I'm peculiar. Most people do."

"No." His gaze on her face held a curious intentness. "I don't think you're peculiar at all. Who is Jacto?"

"My friend. He belongs to one of the tribes in Arnhem Land." Her expression softened. "I've never known anyone as attuned to nature as Jacto. He's very, very old; he reminds me of a baobab tree. No matter how much time passes, or how gnarled and twisted his body becomes, he never really changes. He just conforms and endures."

"You're very fond of him." It was a statement, not a question. No one could mistake the glowing affection in her expression.

"We've been together a long time. I met him six years ago on my trip to Arnhem Land. We just seemed to understand each other. When I left the north, he came with me. He doesn't usually stay anywhere for very long, but he always comes to see me whenever he's nearby."

"Is he with you now?"

She nodded. "I'll introduce you if you like. Why don't you come over to our camp tonight for supper?"

He had to smother an involuntary smile as he noticed how smoothly she had slid in the invitation. "You're clearly adept at making assumptions. I believe you've forgotten that you're supposed to be gone by sundown."

She grinned impishly. "I thought it was worth a try." Her smile faded. "I have to stay, Mr. Gallagher. I'm not here on a whim. I can't tell you how important this is to me."

"Important enough to try to vamp Brent into using his influence?" His lips tightened. "You should have done your homework before accepting his proposition. My actors don't run my set, Miss Delaney."

"Oh, for goodness' sake, couldn't you tell the man

was pulling your leg?" she asked crossly. "I don't sleep with anyone for favors. Brent and I understand each other perfectly."

"I noticed a certain rapport." His tone was caustic. "I underestimated Brent's charm evidently. A few minutes of conversation and you're as dazzled as all his other groupies."

"I am not—" She stopped and drew a deep breath. "Oh, think what you like. It's not important anyway. The only important thing is that you let me stay here until I complete my business." She moistened her lower lip with her tongue. "What difference does it make to you if I stay? Do you still have the crazy idea I'm going to write some kind of exposé and sell it to the press? I never even knew you were coming to Deadman's Ridge until you showed up, but, if it will help, I'll sign anything you like. I'll do anything you like." Her tone lowered to just above a whisper. "Please let me stay."

He couldn't seem to pull his gaze away from her pleading face. Lord, she had lovely amber eyes. Misty and deep, yet alive with feeling. He wanted to keep looking at her for a long, long time. He wanted to reach out and touch her thick curly lashes with the tip of his finger. He wanted her to smile at him again. It was such a little thing she was asking of him. What the hell difference would it make if she stayed around while the shooting was going on? Why not let her . . .

He tore his gaze from her face, his grip tightening on the glass in his hand. She had almost convinced him. In another second he would have yielded to her wide-eyed wistfulness and given her what she wanted. Hell, he was as easy as Brent and Dennis, he thought with disgust. Heaven knows he should know better. "That's a very tempting offer. 'Anything' I like. Did you make the same offer to Brent?"

Manda felt a tiny thrust of pain in her heart. He was iron-hard, suspicious, and had revealed damn few redeeming qualities. She should have been thoroughly disillusioned by now. He certainly shouldn't have been able to hurt her. Yet the pain was there.

"No," she said slowly. "For Pete's sake, can't you think of anything but sex? That wasn't what I meant at all. I just thought maybe I could work part-time for your production company so you wouldn't have to break your damn rule about no outsiders on your precious set. What the devil makes you think you're so damn irresistible that I'd want to jump into bed with you anyway?"

"I'm not fool enough to think any physical charm I might possess could have swept you off your feet," he said dryly. "I know what an ugly bastard I am. I learned a long time ago not to expect women to jump into my bed without—" He broke off. "I know I'm no Brent Penrose. The reasons women come to me are much more basic and practical."

He really believed what he was saying. Manda felt her anger melt away. Did he honestly think women were attracted to him only for what he could give them in the way of material things? Didn't he realize he possessed a greater sexual charisma than Brent could ever have? "You're wrong, you know," she said softly.

"Am I?" His lips twisted cynically. "I've been told that before, but it usually ends the same. I don't mind paying, but I hate lies. You might find it helpful to remember that in our future dealings."

"Future dealings? You've decided to let me stay?"

He hadn't realized until he'd said the words that

he had decided to let her stay. Hell, why should he let Brent have her? He had never wanted anyone as much as he wanted Manda Delaney. If she wasn't what she represented herself to be, why should he care? He was used to dealing with deceitful people. He put his glass down on the ceramic counter with great precision and came slowly toward her. "On certain conditions. I've decided I don't like the idea of Brent having you for a playmate. I want you for myself. No Brent. Do you understand? When I want your company, I'll send someone for you and you'll come running." He smiled as he reached out and touched her cheek with one finger. "I may want only a few hours of relaxing conversation in the evening." He took a step closer and his hard muscular thighs were pressed against her naked legs. She inhaled sharply as she felt his bold arousal. His hands cupped her hips, holding her firmly, letting her feel how much he desired her. "Or I may want this." He moved his hips slowly against her. "I may want to take off every stitch of clothing you're wearing. I may want you to open your thighs and take me into you. I was thinking about that last night while I was lying in bed."

Her gaze was fixed in helpless fascination on the pulse that was jumping in the hollow of his throat. The scent of musk, perspiration, and a cologne containing a hint of leather made her dizzy.

"I didn't want to think about you, but I did. I thought about how tight you'd be around me. I wondered how your breasts would taste. I could visualize your bending over and letting me take . . ."

"Please. You shouldn't say those things." She could barely force the words from her throat.

"Why not? I think it excites you. I can please you,

Manda. I may not be handsome, but I'm very experienced; I can make it good for you."

Once again she felt aching sympathy for him. She wanted to reach up and pull his head down to her shoulder and rock him as if he were a small boy. How crazy to experience sudden maternal tenderness through a haze of hot hunger.

She drew a deep breath. "Yes, it does excite me." She stepped back. "But I'm not a whore, Roman. *If* I go to bed with you, it will be because I want you and for no other reason. Oh, I'm ready to bargain with you to let me stay. You want me to come running? I'll come running. I'll fix your dinner and keep you company. I may let you touch me, and I may not. That depends on how persuasive you can be. In short, I'll let you court me."

"*Court* you?"

"Oh, don't be afraid that I'm trying to trap you into marriage. I don't think marriage would suit me at all."

"Indeed." He smiled dryly. "What a great relief."

"But I *will* be courted, Roman." She met his gaze with her clear, direct one. "I'm not going to let you spoil it. This is the first time it's happened to me, and we're going to do it right." She frowned. "I only wish I had more time to devote to our relationship, but we'll just have to make do."

He was staring at her with an expression that combined wariness with stunned surprise. "May I ask what the hell you're talking about?"

She smiled serenely. "I believe I'm in love with you, Roman."

"What!"

"Oh, it was a surprise to me too. I always thought

love at first sight was pure fantasy. And no one can say you're a likely candidate."

"Do you think I don't know that?"

She wrinkled her nose at him. "And not because you don't look like a bloody movie star. I've always preferred character to good looks anyway. No, it's because you're suspicious, and arrogant, and surly as the devil." She sighed. "However, I'm usually a pretty good judge of character, so somewhere beneath that steel-spiked crust of yours, there must be an extraordinary human being. I'll just have to peel off the layers and find him." She turned toward the door. "It may even be exciting. I've always enjoyed a challenge."

"You're not fooling me, you know." His tone was harsh. "I don't know why you'd think I'd swallow a story like that. I've been conned by experts."

"Have you, Roman?" The glance she threw him over her shoulder was warm with sympathy and tenderness. "I'm sorry to hear that, but I'll never try to con you." She paused. "Tell me you want me to stay. I want to hear you say it."

He scowled. "Hell no, I don't—" He stopped and glared at her. "Why should I want you to stay? You're not promising me one damn thing, and you'll probably be a headache from start to finish."

"But I did make you a promise. I've promised I'll come running. I've promised I'll give you a chance to seduce me." She smiled beguilingly. "And I think you're a man who likes a challenge too."

He was silent for a moment, still scowling at her. Then he said slowly, grudgingly, "Stay."

She laughed softly with genuine humor as she opened the door. "Your graciousness touches me deeply. I can see we're going to—oh, hi, Dennis."

She smiled at the pilot as he stepped aside to let her descend the three steps to the ground. "Roman's just turned down my invitation for an elegant supper alfresco. Care to join Jacto and me?"

"Why not? I've never minded being second choice," Dennis drawled. "And Jacto promised me last night he'd show me how to throw a boomerang. I've been trying for years to learn the skill and never have been able to get the hang of it."

"I remember. I believe I'll disappear down a mine shaft until you've finished your lesson." She lifted her hand in farewell. "Sundown."

"Right." Dennis watched her as she walked briskly away, then turned and mounted the steps. "I've received word that the Cessna will be delivered tomorrow, Roman. Do you want to plan the itinerary for delivering the rushes to the studio in Sydney?"

Roman didn't answer. His gaze was also on Manda's departing figure.

A faint smile touched Dennis's lips. "You're letting her stay?"

Roman didn't take his gaze from Manda. "Yes."

Dennis chuckled. "I thought you would. When Manda starts singing her siren's song, it takes a hard man to say no to her."

"You're speaking about her as if she were some sort of Lorelei."

"Lorelei?" Dennis's brow wrinkled thoughtfully. "I guess there are similarities. She's a persuasive little devil." He closed the door behind him. "But there's no evil in her. She just has so much energy and enthusiasm, she sort of sweeps you along whether you want to go or not." He shook his head. "You know how I've always been afraid of water? When we were in Tasmania, Manda decided it would be the most exciting thing in the world to shoot the Franklin Rapids. None of us in the geology team wanted to go with her. Well, by the time she finished painting verbal pictures of the glories of nature and of white water rafting, we had to get two rafts to hold everyone. And *I* volunteered to be in the first raft."

"Impressive." Not only impressive but dangerous. A woman who had that kind of power over people was seldom shy about using it to her advantage. Dennis was obviously besotted with her, and she'd captivated Brent in the flicker of an eye. Well, he wouldn't be such easy prey. She had caught him off guard with her last remarks, but in retrospect he appreciated what a clever move it was. She had turned the tables on him, received permission to stay, and adjusted the bargain to suit her own terms. She probably doubted he believed her claim of love, but had been sharp enough to realize the value of using shock tactics. She had also been perceptive enough to realize the gauntlet she had thrown down would appeal to him.

"Just what do you know about her, Dennis? She said she was working toward a geology degree. Is that true?"

Something flickered across the older man's face before he lifted his shoulders in a shrug. "As far as I know it's true. I've run into Manda a few times on geologically oriented projects, but she's something of a jill of all trades. According to what she's told me, she's tried her hand at selling, been a seaman on a freighter to Tahiti, written a column for a small weekly paper in Christ Church, driven a taxi in—"

"Wait a minute." Roman's eyes narrowed. "She's written for a newspaper?"

Dennis nodded. "Now, don't get paranoid, Roman. Like I said, it was a very small weekly."

"Out of small acorns . . ." Roman murmured. "Perhaps the lady has ambitions in that direction."

Dennis frowned. "Roman, I don't—"

Roman cut him off with an impatient gesture. "You don't have to defend her. I don't give a damn if she's a newspaper reporter or not. I've just always found it's a good idea to know precisely with whom I'm dealing."

For an instant Roman experienced a queer sensation of pain, and then it was gone. What had he expected, for heaven's sake? Manda Delaney was probably a world-class expert at weaving the emotional magic she had displayed that afternoon. Yet perhaps deep down he had wanted her honesty and glowing joie de vivre to be genuine. It would have been good to know that somewhere in this weary, cynical world those qualities still existed.

As he had told Dennis, it didn't really matter whether she was a Delilah or not. He would use her as she intended to use him. It had been a long time since any woman had posed a challenge to him. It might be interesting to find out how long a "courtship" it would take to bring her to his bed. He turned away. "I'll be with you in a minute, Dennis. I need to shower and change. Help yourself to a drink."

"Dennis is coming to dinner, Jacto. He said you promised to teach him how to throw a boomerang." Manda sat down in the shade under the canvas awning of the lean-to. The intense heat wavered before her eyes in visible rays. For a moment she thought wistfully of the coolness of Roman's mobile home. Then she dismissed the thought firmly. It would be even hotter in the mine, and drawing comparisons would only make it worse. "Do you think you can keep him amused? I'm going to have to start working in the new tunnel this afternoon, so I can stop only briefly for dinner."

"You slept very little last night," Jacto observed. "It would be best if you took a nap now and worked when the sun went down."

"No time. I may have to spend a few hours every evening over at the production set from now on, and that's bound to interfere with my schedule. I'll just have to work harder when I get the chance." She sat up and reached for the canteen beside the bedroll. "Well, there's no use putting it off. Once more into the breach."

"I don't believe *Henry the Fifth* is appropriate in this case."

She should have realized Jacto would recognize the quote. As far as she knew, he was entirely self-educated and amazingly well-informed. *He* was amazing. She had been tempted many times to ask how he had acquired his knowledge, since he grew up in a period when his race had been cruelly downtrodden. She always dismissed the idea as soon as it came; Jacto didn't encourage questions about either his past or his future.

"Don't quibble," she said lightly. "It's appropriate when taken out of context." She lit the lantern and drew on the leather gloves that protected her hands from the rubble she was forced to handle. "Now, I've got to see if the ladder is safe. It was sagging horribly the last time I went down."

"It is safe. I fixed the ladder and went down into the new tunnel while you were gone." He smiled faintly. "There's much rubble and dust but no snakes this time."

She shivered. "That's a relief." In the first tunnel she had discovered an entire family of black snakes which they had to remove before she could begin her search. After that, every time she had moved a board or a rock she had expected to see another slithering reptile. It hadn't made the search any easier on her nerves. "Thanks, Jacto. I wasn't looking forward to the first trip down into the tunnel."

"I will call you when supper is ready. You will want to bathe in the billabong first?"

She nodded. "The water always feels like heaven to me after being underground for hours." She stepped from the shade out into the sunlight and inhaled sharply as the full force of the heat struck her. "Is the tunnel long?"

"Longer than the last one." Jacto's ink-black gaze was suddenly on her face. "What if you do not find the pouch? What will you do then?"

"I *have* to find it. The pouch has to be here in Deadman's Ridge. Charlie wrote to his wife just before he was murdered, and told her that he was putting the Black Flame in a pouch within a pouch and hiding it somewhere safe."

"A pouch *within* a pouch?"

She shrugged. "Opals shatter easily. He probably wanted to cushion it."

"You told me there have been many searches by other members of your family and no opal has been found. It would be reasonable to assume that Charles Delaney may have fabricated the story."

"No! It's here. I *know* it's here." Her hand clenched on the handle of the lantern. "Why are you doing this, Jacto? I have enough pressure on me without having you doubt me too."

Jacto's expression didn't change. "I do not doubt you. But it is wise to remember no matter how much we desire something, sometimes we must accept a lesser prize. And the prize we win may not always be what we believe it to be."

"The Black Flame will be everything Charlie said it was," Manda said with a touch of desperation in her voice. "It has to be."

"I'm not talking of that prize, Manda."

"Oh, Lord, you're at it again." She laughed huskily as she turned away. "Most of the time I don't know what in the world you're talking about, Jacto."

"You will, when the time comes." He picked up his pipe, put it in his mouth, and drew on it deeply. "Be sure you drink plenty of water and take your salt tablets while you're down there."

"I will." She could feel Jacto's gaze on her back as she walked the few yards to the open mine shaft. It was clear Jacto was in one of his savant moods. She should have been accustomed to him by now, she thought, but he still was able to unsettle her on occasion. Not that she wasn't unsettled enough already. She had been buoyed up with ebullient confidence when she had left Roman, but now she was being bombarded by doubts. He was a hard man, and heaven knows *she* wasn't the least bit hard. What had made her think she could be intimate with him and come out the winner?

The sexual chemistry between them had been so explosive that she had almost melted into a puddle on the floor of the trailer. And he had scarcely touched her. It would take all her control to keep from jumping into bed with him when he snapped his fingers, but she knew she mustn't give in too soon. She had to have time enough to forge a deeper relationship before sex entered the picture. Sometime in his past, Roman had obviously been badly hurt, and a sexual encounter now had only the shallowest meaning for him. There was no way she would permit him to look upon their coming together as a shallow or unimportant occurrence.

She carefully negotiated the ladder, holding the lantern in her left hand to light the way into the darkness below. Well, one challenge at a time. Right now she had to concentrate all her attention on the challenge presented in finding the Black Flame.

Three

"It's been two days," Manda said cheerfully as soon as Roman opened the door. "I was beginning to think you'd changed your mind until Mark, here, arrived with your note." She grinned engagingly at the freckle-faced young man who had accompanied her to Roman's trailer. "I'll see you tomorrow, Mark."

He nodded eagerly. "I'll be over as soon as I finish working on the set. What should I wear?"

"As little as possible. It's hot as Hades down there."

"Right. I'm looking forward to it."

Roman watched the boy as he walked away. "Another conquest?" he asked dryly.

"He's never been down in an opal mine." Manda climbed the metal steps and closed the door behind her. "I told him I'd take him down and let him look around." She closed her eyes and gave a delicious shiver. "It feels absolutely wonderful in here. Sometimes I forget there's such a thing as coolness in the world." She lifted her eyelids to reveal eyes that were dancing with mischief. "You'll notice that I came running as you commanded, O Glorious Potentate. I didn't even stop to wash up." She ran her fingers through her hair, which was darkened by dust and perspiration. "But I've got to do it within the next five minutes or I won't be able to stand myself. May I use your shower?" She held up a small canvas tote bag. "I brought a change of clothes and my own towel."

"Pity. The idea of you naked and dependent on me for even a towel had definite possibilities." He gestured toward the door leading to the bath. "By all means, use anything you like. If you need any help, you only have to call."

Manda's heart was pounding fast, and she found it hard to breathe. She had forgotten in the last two days how intense her physical reaction to Roman was. His thick dark hair was slightly damp from the shower, and she could detect the delicious scent of soap and aftershave. She found her gaze kept drifting to the virile dark hair above the top button of his blue shirt. She forced herself to turn away. "I'll keep that in mind. You might pour me something cool, my throat feels as if it's lined with sandpaper." She hesitated and suddenly glanced back over her shoulder. "Why did you wait two days to send for me?"

"I had things to do. If you remember, I have a picture to film. I'm sorry to disillusion you, but you're very low on my list of priorities and—" He broke off in mid-sentence. Her enormous amber eyes were opened wide, and she had a hurt expression on her face. He suddenly felt as if he had wounded a baby antelope. "Oh, for Pete's sake, stop looking at me like that. I didn't want to send for you at all. I'd almost decided I wanted nothing to do with you." He released his breath with harsh explosiveness. "I couldn't stop thinking about you, dammit. Are you satisfied now?"

"Yes." She smiled. "Very satisfied. I couldn't stop thinking about you either. I'll be right back."

When she returned twenty minutes later, she was wearing cut-offs which were faded to a blue-white color by the strong desert sun, and the same low-cut white T-shirt she had worn the first time he had seen her. Her hair was freshly shampooed and combed, and she'd left it to dry in wet strands on her shoulders. Her face had the glowingly well-scrubbed look of a small child.

She padded forward on bare feet and took a glass of iced tea from Roman, uttering a blissful sigh of contentment. "That looks wonderful." She took a sip of the drink. "And it tastes as good as it looks. I'm positively drowning in luxury. A hot shower, a cold drink, and air-conditioning. Could I ask for anything more?"

"I know quite a few women who have asked for a great deal more. You're easily pleased."

"Not really. I'll probably demand a hell of a lot more from you than anyone else would ever dream of asking. Just give me the chance." She took another drink and put the glass down on the bar. "Now, what can I do for you? Do you want me to cook for you or sew a button on your shirt or—"

"I want to look at you. I want to rub against you and see your eyes widen and your tongue moisten your lips as they did the last time. I want to see if it was my imagination or if I really want you as much as I believe I do. Why the hell did you think I sent for you? If I'd wanted a meal, I would have gone to the mess tent. Wardrobe sews on my buttons."

"How convenient." Her voice was trembling. "Well, I'm hungry even if you aren't. Do you mind if I fix myself a sandwich?"

He gazed at her moodily. "Would it matter if I said yes?"

"No. I've been down in the mine shaft all day and it's almost sundown now. I haven't had anything to eat since breakfast." She edged past him into the kitchenette, being careful to avoid touching him. Even though she eluded actual contact with him, she was aware of the heat of his body, and her senses reeled as she once again caught a whiff of the wonderful masculine scent that clung to him. "No civilized human being would deny a hungry woman sustenance."

"Who told you I was civilized?"

"No one had to tell me." She opened the refrigerator door and took out cold cuts and Swiss cheese. "I saw *Fulfillment*. You wrote it as well as directed it." She looked up and smiled at him. "There was nothing uncaring or uncivilized about that motion picture. It was the most exquisitely sensitive portrayal of love I've ever seen. The man who created that beautiful film has to be a very special person."

His gaze searched her face. "I think you really mean it. You're not just stroking my ego."

"Of course I mean it. I don't say things I don't mean. Do you have tomato? Oh, there it is." She reached down into the vegetable crisper and triumphantly pulled out a large tomato. "Maybe I fell in love with the man who wrote those beautiful words before I even saw you. Heaven knows, you haven't done anything since I met you to account for the sudden insane feelings I've developed for you. You've only growled and propositioned and threatened. It's a wonder I haven't given up on you and—" She broke off and turned to look at him. He was laughing. Not just smiling, but *laughing*, and his dark angular face suddenly wasn't unattractive at all. "Did I say something funny?"

He shook his head, his dark eyes dancing. "You were perfectly serious. That's what was so amusing. I wasn't sure whether you were addressing your passionate declaration to me or to my tomato."

She smiled happily at him. His face had softened with laughter and the wariness was gone from his expression. She could feel joy rising within her. It was starting. The great adventure was about to begin. "Well, it's a very fine tomato. Would you like me to slice some for you?"

He slowly shook his head, still gazing bemusedly at her. "Why didn't you eat today?"

"I didn't want to take the time." She opened the bread box on the counter and took out two pieces of rye bread. "I'm working with a deadline."

He stiffened. "What kind of deadline?"

"I have to have my job done in another three weeks." She changed the subject. "What kind of film are you making this time?"

"It's a historical drama about the first opal miners in Australia." His gaze was narrowed on her face. "Just what the hell are you doing here? You can't be mining. Without a license you wouldn't be permitted to keep anything you discovered. Yet you're telling me you're putting in hours of labor down in that mine shaft."

"No, I'm not mining." Dammit, she hated being

evasive with him. "Look, I can't answer you. Okay? It's not only my secret; there are others involved."

"Who?"

She gazed at him in helpless silence. He wasn't smiling any longer, and she couldn't bear to watch the wariness return to his expression. "Please," she whispered. "Trust me. I'd never do anything to hurt you."

"Why the hell should I trust—" He stopped and was silent a moment, looking at her. Then he smiled. "There's some potato salad and cheesecake somewhere in the refrigerator. You need more than a sandwich. You're too thin. Doesn't your friend Jacto make you eat?"

She released her breath shakily, feeling relieved. "Jacto believes everyone should guide his own life."

"Well, evidently you're not doing a terrific job with your steering." He frowned. "Were you working in the mine that first night I saw you?"

She nodded. "It's cooler at night. Sometimes it becomes unbearable during the day." She smiled. "Don't worry. I'm very tough. I've taken on more arduous projects than this in my time."

Arnhem Land, the Franklin Rapids, and who knows where else she had wandered, he thought.

"So Dennis tells me." Roman slowly shook his head. "Why?"

"Why did you travel over every nook and cranny of Australia when you made those documentaries?" Her eyes were glowing softly. "Excitement, adventure, change. No one else seems to understand except Jacto, and perhaps my father. But I believe you might know what I'm talking about, Roman."

His dark eyes flickered to reveal a look of wistful sadness. "Yes, I understand."

At that moment he realized how wrong Dennis had been about Manda. She was no Lorelei, but the fantasy character she did resemble made him ache in sympathy for what was to come. He suddenly wanted to take her in his arms and hold her tenderly. How long had it been since he had felt tenderness toward someone? Yet it was sweeping through him now with a force that made him tremble.

The glow faded from her eyes and was replaced by uncertainty. "Why are you looking at me like that?" She laughed shakily. "You're frightening me."

He smiled and crossed the few feet separating them. His fingers reached out to touch the curve of her cheek with exquisite delicacy. "Not you," he said gently. "You're not one to be frightened easily."

His gaze flowed over her with the same gentleness she felt in his touch. It soothed her like a blanket of satin. Her voice trembled slightly. "Something's happening, isn't it? You're beginning to like me. It's not just sex anymore."

His smile deepened. "It *is* sex, but yes, something else is happening."

"You like me?"

It seemed too weak a word to describe the aching tenderness he was experiencing. "I like you."

She sighed with relief. "Thank goodness. I thought it would take much longer to make a major breakthrough. It would be just my luck to fall in love with an iron-willed man. I've been having nightmares about piercing that hard shell."

"I'm not hard or unfeeling," he said slowly. "Wary, perhaps. I've wished many times I could be hard. It would make my life easier."

"But you'd miss so much," she said earnestly. "And the rest of the world would miss out on some lovely experiences, like seeing *Fulfillment*. A hard man would never have been able to create a film of such depth and beauty." She took a deep breath and looked directly into his eyes. "I'd rather not go to bed with you immediately, if you don't mind."

His eyes widened in surprise. "I beg your pardon?"

"Naturally, if you insist, I won't object, but . . ."

He was laughing. "You make me dizzy. One minute you're throwing down challenges, and the next minute you're offering to jump into bed with me if I crook my finger." The amusement faded from his face. "Why?"

Wariness clouded his expression again, and Manda felt a sudden pang of tenderness. What experiences had bred the distrust that now was a part of him? "Because I'm in love with you, and I don't believe in holding anything back if you love someone. I posed the challenge only to make sure you wouldn't kick me out after you'd had your wicked way with me. But you *like* me now."

"That could be a very dangerous philosophy." His tone had turned suddenly harsh. "And how in the devil could you fall in love with me? You don't even know what kind of man I am. I wouldn't have broken my word about letting you stay, but I was sure as hell ready to use you."

"I know," she said simply. "It doesn't matter. I've always trusted my instincts, and I don't see why I should stop now. There must be some reason why I feel so strongly about you. Jacto says all things in nature have a reason for being."

"I think I'm going to have to meet this Jacto."

"You will." She grinned up at him eagerly. "I want

you to meet everyone I care about. My father, my sisters, and I have so many friends you'd like—"

He held up his hand to stop her words. "I'm not about to let you take me home to meet your family." There was a touch of exasperation in his tone. "Dammit, I don't love you, and I will *not* be swept away by your zealous emotions." He pronounced every word deliberately. "Liking is not loving, Manda."

"But it's a start. You'll find I can be very lovable. I tend to grow on people. And you don't have to worry about meeting my family yet. There are reasons why that wouldn't be practical now." She stopped to get her breath. "Well, do we go to bed together or not? I'd appreciate the chance to get to know you better, but it's up to you. I'm sure it would be very enjoyable."

"I appreciate your confidence in my sexual prowess." A tiny smile tugged at his lips. "I feel as if I've been inspected and just received a government stamp of approval."

"What do I need with a government stamp of approval? I told you I relied on my own instincts." She moistened her lips with her tongue. "Well?"

Her tone was filled with apprehension, and he felt a poignant, aching tenderness toward her again. "I wouldn't want you to be disillusioned regarding my 'exquisite sensitivity.'"

She hurled herself into his arms and hugged him tightly. "Oh, thank you, Roman. It won't be long, I promise. I don't know why I'm so nervous."

Her soft full breasts were pressed against his chest and he could feel the hard pointed pressure of her nipples through the thin layers of cloth that separated them. He inhaled deeply, trying to force oxygen into his suddenly constricted lungs. The muscles of his stomach knotted painfully. He gently pushed her away. "If you want me to wait more than a minute, I think you'd better avoid touching me. My control isn't in top shape at the moment. Why don't you finish making your sandwich?"

"All right." She began to prepare her sandwich. She had thrown herself into Roman's arms with her usual impulsiveness, she realized, but she doubted if she'd ever be so casual again. Her body had reacted to their brief contact as if she had connected with an electric wire. "I noticed you have a mobile phone and that there's a radio operator in the shed by the mess tent. I wonder if you'd let me phone my sisters later and give them your call number? Otherwise I'll have to drive my Jeep into Coober Pedy every few days to keep in touch with them. I promise they won't bother you except in a case of an emergency."

He nodded absently, his gaze on the fluctuating color in her cheeks. "Of course. You're close to your sisters?"

"Yes." She looked up, an affectionate smile on her face. "We're as different as the seasons, but we couldn't be closer. I guess growing up on Killaroo was responsible for that. We didn't have any other playmates for most of our childhood, so we had to learn to get along."

"Killaroo?"

"Our sheep station in New South Wales. It's been in our family for generations. I'd like you to see it." Her eyes were glowing with warmth. "It's so beautiful."

He smiled. "More beautiful than Arnhem Land or the Franklin Rapids?"

"No, but Killaroo is . . . different." She finished simply, "Killaroo is home. Where's home for you?"

His expression immediately became blank. "I was

born in Perth." He moved across the room to the refrigerator. "I'll get the cheesecake for you."

He might as well have posted a No Trespassing sign, she thought sadly. But she had no reason to complain. They had become closer in the short time they'd shared together than she would have dreamed possible. His about-face had come so abruptly, it had made her a little uneasy. What had triggered his sudden reversal? She had seen something in his face. . . . She instinctively shied away from that line of thought. She was probably imagining it anyway. She would try to stop worrying and just enjoy their relationship. "Cut a piece for yourself. I don't like to eat alone. I don't like to do anything alone."

"Don't you? I could have guessed that about you." He took the cheesecake out of the refrigerator. "Don't worry. I won't let you be alone."

"There was someone watching you last night."

Manda's gaze rose swiftly from the map of the mine which was spread out on the ground in front of her to rest on Jacto's face. "Who?"

"I do not know. I saw footprints and four cigarette butts by the ghost gum tree at the billabong." He nodded at a bleach-barked tree several hundred yards away. "He stayed a very long time. First standing, and then squatting."

"Are you—" She broke off. Of course he was sure. Jacto was a wonderful tracker. "Someone from the film company?"

He shrugged. "Who else? Do not worry. I'll find out tonight who he is and we will be on our guard against him."

"No." Her tone was sharp. Jacto was deadly with a boomerang and a hunting knife, but he was still an old man. The thought that someone would come down to their camp in the middle of the night to keep them under surveillance was icily menacing. "It was probably somebody with an overdeveloped curiosity who wanted to see what we were up to."

Jacto looked at her skeptically without answering. He knew as well as she what a fever prospecting for opals generated in some individuals. How many murders had taken place on this very ridge over the years? There was no reason why things should be any different now. Time passed, but human nature remained the same.

She ruffled her hair wearily. "For heaven's sake, the field is played out. Do they think I'm going to make a major strike?"

"You work very hard. It's reasonable to think there is a purpose for such effort." He smiled faintly. "And you know many fine opals have been found in supposedly played-out mines."

"Just throw your hat over your shoulder and dig where it lands," she quoted with a grimace. "You know, I'm almost tempted to try to find my own Black Flame while I'm down in that shaft. It would be a hell of a lot less exasperating than looking for Charlie's. But, unfortunately, forty-five-carat opals don't turn up every day or even every century." Her attention returned to the map. "There are only two more tunnels. I should be through with this one by the end of the week." She rubbed the back of her neck tiredly. "You know, I found something sad down there. There are drawings on the walls of this tunnel. Nothing elaborate. Just sketches of birds and trees. Sort of like the ones your ancestors made in the caves at Kakadu. Some of them are just broken remnants where a miner has mutilated them drilling for opals. They have to be Charlie's work. According to Mignon's journal, Charlie was an artist and he wanted the opal money only so he could go to Paris and study. Can't you imagine him down there, painting by lantern light, trying to escape from the violence and greed of Deadman's Ridge?" She shook her head sadly. "But the violence found him anyway. I guess I've been thinking of Charlie as a phantom figure, even a caricature, but lately he's come alive for me. Do you know he was only twenty-six years old when he was murdered? That's only two years older than I am right now. He had a wife and a child and he wanted to *live*. When I discovered that first painting of a bowerbird, I felt like howling like a baby." She laughed shakily. "Lord, I sound stupid."

"You are only tired." He glanced away. "You are going to Gallagher again tonight?"

"As soon as I get enough energy to move. It's so humid I can't breathe."

"It will soon be better. It will rain before sundown."

Sundown was only an hour away, and there wasn't a sign of a cloud in the pale white-blue of the sky, but she didn't question the statement. If Jacto said there would be rain, there would be rain. "That will be a relief. Maybe it'll cool things off a little." She folded the map and tucked it into her knapsack. "Why don't you come with me tonight? I want you to meet Roman, and you could use a hearty meal."

"No."

She sighed. Jacto was acting very peculiar lately. In the past three days since Roman had sent for her, he had stubbornly refused to go with her to the encampment to meet Roman. There appeared to be no animosity in his refusal, he just didn't seem to want to have anything to do with the man.

"I'll bring you something then. I'll be back before ten." She suddenly frowned. "And don't you go looking for our snoop while I'm gone."

His black eyes were limpid. "Why would an old man like me go out in the rain and risk a chill? As you say, perhaps there is no danger."

"Jacto . . ." She could tell by his expression he wouldn't be swayed by anything she could say. She could only hope the rain would discourage any intruders. "Oh, do you what you like. You will anyway, dammit."

"You always were a wise child."

A reluctant smile curved her lips as she glanced at his bland face over her shoulder. "I'm almost twenty-four years old. I'm not the eighteen-year-old kid you met in Arnhem Land six years ago."

"You are older, but you are still that child." For an instant there was a flicker of the same melancholy she had seen in Roman's expression three days ago. "For now."

She laughed as she shook her head. "I'll always be a child to you, Jacto." She waved. "Take care of yourself. I'll bring you some of Roman's espresso."

Her smile gradually faded as she crossed the field toward the encampment in the distance. Roman was filming beyond the west ridge today, and the location appeared deserted. All of a sudden, she felt very much alone in the stark silence of the vast desolation surrounding her. She could now see a faint darkening of the sky as storm clouds began to roll across the horizon from the west.

It wasn't the only storm that was gathering in her life, she thought. Sexual tension had been crackling between Roman and her with electric force for the last three days, and an explosion was imminent. She found herself torn between eager excitement and a strange, uncharacteristic feeling of shyness. She had believed she would get over her initial nervousness once she got to know Roman better, but spending time with him had done little to alleviate it.

She was happy she'd had some breathing space, however, and all she had learned of Roman was infinitely reassuring. Beneath his facade of harsh cynicism was a man with entirely different qualities. He could be gentle, and he was both perceptive and brilliant. In fact, he was everything she wanted in a man. He handled his crew with intelligence, decisiveness, and the saving grace of a dry sense of humor. She knew now that he had a passion for poker, an obsession for his chosen profession, and more patience than she had first given him credit for. Yet everything she had learned about him concerned the present. He never mentioned either his family or his past.

Well, what could she expect? She hadn't been able to be entirely open with him either. She had been tempted many times to break the agreement she had made with her sisters, Sydney and Addie, and tell him why she was in Deadman's Ridge, but she had always changed her mind at the last minute. The bond she was forging with Roman was very new and fragile. The bond that bound her to Sydney and Addie had roots formed through a lifetime of trust and love. She could never betray that trust, not even for Roman.

She heard a throbbing sound, and her head lifted eagerly. Sound carried uncannily in this vast waste-land, and the hum of a Jeep motor could be heard for many miles. Her gaze searched the west ridge, where the purple-black clouds were now a solid bank on its horizon. Her heart was suddenly pounding with anticipation. She couldn't see him yet, but she knew he was coming. Her steps quickened as she moved toward the gleaming silver mobile home in the encampment. He was coming!

Four

She ran to meet him as his Jeep pulled to a stop by the trailer. "There's going to be a storm."

"I know." Roman was frowning as he stepped out of the Jeep. "That's why we had to pack up and come back early. Dammit, we had another hour of shooting to do."

"I've never seen a storm in the desert." Her amber eyes were incandescent with excitement. "Have you?"

"Once or twice." His frown was replaced by an indulgent smile as he looked at her glowing face. "Do you mean there's actually something you haven't experienced?"

"All sorts of things. But I still have plenty of time." She jumped into the passenger seat of the Jeep. "Come on. Let's go to meet it."

"We have to ride on a dirt road. We'll be lucky if we don't mire down and get stuck overnight."

"I don't care." She lifted her hand and ran her fingers through her hair. The breeze that touched her cheeks was moist and cool and scented pun gently with spinifix and the eucalyptus of the ghost gum trees. "I want to be there. And I want you to be there with me. Please, Roman."

A faint smile touched his lips. "I must be crazy. I'm tired and hungry. . . ." He stepped back into the Jeep and started the ignition. "And I'm going with you."

Her laughter pealed out joyously. "I knew you would. You're going to enjoy it as much as I will."

His grin became reckless. "You're damn right I will."

He backed up and turned the Jeep, lifting his hand in a mocking salute as he passed another Jeep occupied by Brent and Dennis that was just pulling into the encampment. "Even if my entire production team does think I've gone bonkers." He stomped on the accelerator and the Jeep leaped forward.

It was wonderful! The speed of the Jeep, the roughness of the road beneath their wheels, the moist wind tearing at her hair. Lightning pierced the roiling dark clouds with tinsel flares of silver. She felt as if they were alone in the world. Pure desolation surrounded them on all sides, and yet she had never felt more vibrantly alive.

She suddenly jumped to her feet, gripping the windshield tightly with both hands. Without the protective barrier of the windshield, the force of the wind was painful, as if it were trying to rip her hair from her scalp.

"For heaven's sake, sit down. If we hit a bump, you'll be tossed out." Roman reached out with one hand and jerked her back onto her seat. He was laughing, too, his dark eyes shining with the same wild exhilaration she was feeling.

"I love it," she shouted over the roar of the wind and the motor. "Oh, I love it, Roman."

"I know you do."

"And you love it too. I can see you do. *Say* it, Roman."

"I love it," he shouted, and his laughter rang out over the desert and joined with the wind and the thunder.

The rain suddenly poured from the sky in sheets, drenching them both in seconds and turning the road into a cinnamon-brown stream.

It was all wonderful. The stinging wildness of the rain only added to the excitement of the moment. "Let's go on forever. I never want to stop—" She broke off as the Jeep swerved and then skidded crazily across the road.

It was over in a second, and Roman had the Jeep under control again. His breath was coming in shuddering gasps as his hands clutched the steering wheel with white-knuckled force. His dark hair was plastered to his forehead and drops of rain were running down his cheeks and into the open collar of his shirt. "That's it." He turned the wheel ninety degrees. "It's over. We're going back to camp."

"No, I want—"

"We're going back," he interrupted harshly. "Dammit, the Jeep could have overturned back there. I could have *killed* you, and you still want to go on."

She laughed softly. Her face was being washed by the spring rain, her hair was wet and felt gloriously wild and free, and Roman had been so worried about her he had turned pale and shouted at her. To know Roman cared that much for her was even more wonderful than the experience of driving through the storm. "All right, we'll go back. You don't have to get so uptight about it."

"Uptight! Dammit, you—" He stopped and drew a deep breath. "Look, just be quiet until we get back to camp, will you? I'm having enough trouble keeping this blasted Jeep on the road without worrying about holding on to my temper too."

"Whatever you say." Her lashes lowered demurely to veil the mischief in her eyes. "I certainly didn't mean to upset you."

He cast her a glowering look and muttered a curse beneath his breath.

Dennis was coming out of the mess tent as they drove into the encampment, and he made a face as the Jeep splattered muddy water on the bottoms of his khaki trousers. "Blast it, Roman, I'm already wet to the skin. You didn't have to give me a mud bath."

Roman pulled the Jeep up in front of his mobile home and turned off the ignition. "Sorry," he said tersely. "I suggest you stay inside if you don't want to get splattered. The whole damn desert is a bloody swamp."

Dennis lifted a sandy brow. "Peevish, aren't we? I wanted to see you as soon as you came back. How the hell do you expect me to get four camels into my Cessna? It's not a blasted transport plane, you know."

Roman frowned. "Don't be an ass. I didn't say you had to fly in the camels. They're going to be trucked overland from Sydney. Who said I wanted you to—" He stopped. "Don't tell me. Brent Penrose."

Dennis nodded. "I should have known he was putting me on." His gaze shifted to Manda, who was shaking with laughter. "You don't have to enjoy it so damn much."

"Sorry, Dennis." She jumped from the Jeep and ran over to him, giving him a quick kiss on the cheek. "I just had a picture of you crowded in that six-seat Cessna playing baby-sitter to four camels." She went off again into gales of laughter and whirled him in a circle before releasing him. "Besides, I feel good. Isn't this a wonderful day?"

The thunder was still rumbling, the rain was still falling, and they were all soaked. Yet Dennis found himself nodding as he stared bemusedly at her luminous face. "A fine day if you're a duck."

"But I'm not a duck." She spun away from him, her arms outstretched as if she were about to fly. "I'm a swan. Have I told you how much my sister Sydney loves swans, Roman?"

"No." He was gazing at her with the same bemused expression as Dennis.

"Well, she does." She whirled in a circle. "Black swans."

"Your feathers are getting sodden, Madame Swan," Roman said gruffly. "Suppose you run inside and let them dry."

She smiled brilliantly. "Okay." She leaped up the metal steps and disappeared into the interior of the mobile home.

Both men gazed after her in silence for a long moment.

Dennis chuckled. "Didn't I tell you she was a bloody Lorelei?"

Roman slowly shook his head, his heavy lids shadowing his eyes. "No, you were wrong. She's no Lorelei." He moved around the Jeep toward the trailer. "She's Peter Pan."

● ● ●

As Manda came out of the bathroom dabbing at her wet hair with a large white towel, Roman walked in. She tossed him the other towel she had draped over her arm.

"I thought you'd want to dry your feathers too. We're both so wet we're making puddles. What's this about camels?"

He caught the towel and began to wipe the moisture running down his face from his wet hair. "I want the picture to be as authentic as possible, and quite a few of the gold and opal miners used camels instead of donkeys and horses as pack animals." He smiled. "I don't blame Dennis for being upset at the idea of sharing his precious Cessna with those animals. They're notoriously bad-tempered, and even their trainer has a problem putting them through their paces. Dennis is probably tracking Brent down now to get even with him for his little joke."

"How is Brent doing? Are you happy with him?"

His expression became wary. "Why do you ask? Have you decided to reconsider his offer after all?" A savage emotion flickered in the depths of his dark eyes. "Well, you can forget it. I may not be as pretty as Penrose, but you'll have to make do. There's no way I'm going to let you go now."

Her eyes widened in surprise. Her question had been perfectly innocent, and she'd had no idea it would initiate such a violent reaction. "For Pete's sake, I only asked how he was performing, not for permission to climb into his bed." She raised her chin. "Not that I would have asked anyway. I run my life to suit myself, Roman."

He scowled. "You don't have to tell me that. Wandering around the country like a bloody swagman, running rapids and . . ." His scowl deepened. "What the hell is so amusing?"

"It just struck me funny that you compared me to a hobo. Do you know what my name is?"

"Manda Delaney."

She shook her head. "Matilda. My father named me for the unofficial national anthem. He's the most patriotic Aussie I've ever met. My two sisters were luckier. He only named them after principal cities, Sydney and Adelaide." She wrinkled her nose. "But what kid could bear a name like Matilda? When I was six, I dug in my heels and announced that in the future Matilda would not exist. There would only be Manda."

The fierceness gradually faded from Roman's face. "I'd say that was more than enough."

She nodded. "I was a handful."

"You still are." He crossed the room toward her. "Bend over and let me dry your hair. You're just dabbing at it."

She obediently bent over, and he immediately enveloped her head with the towel. He began to rub briskly with far more thoroughness than gentleness. "Ouch! I feel like a lamb being shorn."

"Stop grousing. I'm trying to keep you from getting pneumonia."

"And enjoying every minute of it." She was silent for a moment, then asked thoughtfully, "You're still angry with me, aren't you?"

His hands hesitated before he resumed rubbing. "Probably."

"Why? You're not being reasonable."

His words were so low they were muffled through the towel. "I'm jealous as hell, and jealous men aren't known to be reasonable." She tried to raise her head. "Be still. Let me finish with this."

"I want to see your face."

"You can delay that aesthetic treat," he said bitterly.

"Roman . . . I don't understand. You're one of the most secure people I've ever met. Jealousy isn't an emotion I'd attribute to you."

"There are times when I'm not at all secure. You'd better learn that fact now. I can be jealous and possessive and more uncivilized than you could imagine. Some of the things I feel on the inside are just as ugly as what you see on the outside."

She fought free of the towel, and looked up at him. "You're not—"

"Don't lie." His eyes were blazing down at her. "I know what I look like. I accepted it a long time ago. I just wanted you to know you have to be careful." He threw the towel aside, and she was suddenly in his arms. "Because you're one of the things I've found I can't be civilized about."

His lips covered hers with so much hard passion that her lungs were robbed of breath and her knees of strength. Heat. She felt a throbbing heat that defied reality. As her breasts pressed against his hard chest, they became excruciatingly sensitive. His lips moved to her throat and he kissed the cord of her neck. He shuddered, his muscles coiled with tension. "I want to drive into you and never come out," he muttered. His tongue moved yearningly against her throat. "I want to crush you and— Tell me to stop. I want to *hurt* you, dammit."

His voice was so intense it rocked through her. "I don't want you to stop." She pressed closer and felt another shudder ripple through him. "But I also don't want you to make love to me in anger. Why do you want to hurt me?"

"Go away." His arms tightened around her even as

he said the words. "I don't want this. I don't want anyone to have the power to churn me up and turn me inside out." His next words were halting and muffled in her hair. "I'm scared as hell. I guess I want to strike out before you come too near. I don't want to give anyone the power to hurt me."

Manda could feel tears sting her eyes as a melting tenderness inundated every particle of her being. His confession had been raw and clumsy and poignantly touching. "I'll never hurt you. I only want you to love me. Please trust me."

He pushed her away to look down into her face; his was taut and pale, his jaw clenched, the jagged white scar on his cheekbone becoming more prominent. "I think I'm going to have to." His voice was thick with emotion. "But heaven help you if you betray me, Manda. I don't know what I'd do to you if I found—"

Her fingers swiftly covered his lips. "No threats," she whispered. "No violence. Just love me."

His eyes were still dark with torment as he slowly opened his lips and captured her fingers in his mouth. He sucked gently, his warm tongue outlining each finger.

She couldn't get her breath; her breasts rose and fell as if she were running. The movement of his tongue was lighting tiny fires inside her that were spreading into her bloodstream and melting muscle and bone in their wake.

The torment was now gone from his eyes, replaced by a smoky sensuality. He reached up and slowly pulled her fingers from his mouth, his teeth gently serrating her flesh, his tongue both soothing and teasing. "I love the way you taste. I'm going to have to sample more of you." He nipped lightly at the tip of her index finger. "Much more."

She tried to think of something to say, but her mind was a haze of heat and sensation. She could only stare up at him helplessly.

His hands moved to the side button of her khaki shorts. "You're wet. Let's get these clothes off you." His fingers were trembling as they moved to the zipper and slowly slid it down. "Are you cold?"

"No." She barely managed to get the word past the tightness in her throat. "Hurry."

"I don't want to hurry." His gaze was fixed on her full breasts which were outlined in bold detail by the wet cotton of her T-shirt. "For the last five nights I've been lying awake thinking about all I want to do with you. I don't know if I can pull it off, but I want to do everything in slow motion." He tugged the shirt out of her shorts and pulled it over her head. Then his fingers went to the front closure of her bra and slowly unfastened it. "I've never seen a more beautiful sight than you standing up in that Jeep with your hair flying around you and the look on your face as if you wanted to make love to the whole damn world." He slid the straps of her bra carefully down her arms. His eyes fastened on her naked breasts, and his breathing became shallow and strained. "I wanted to stop the Jeep and rip your clothes off in the middle of the wind and the rain. I was hurting so bad I thought it would kill me." His fingers slowly unbuttoned his ivory-colored shirt, and he shrugged out of it. "All I could think about was how you would feel around me. Silky and tight and . . . Come *here*." He pulled her to him.

She inhaled sharply. Sensations she'd never experienced before assaulted her with stunning force.

The thatch of dark curly hair on his chest was pressed against her sensitive breasts, his strong, heavily muscled thighs were suddenly on either side of her own, and his arousal was insinuated against the center of her womanhood. She was surrounded by the scent of soap and the erotic musky aroma of his maleness.

"Do you want me?" His voice was harsh. "I'm going crazy. If you don't really want me, you'd better tell me now." His heart was drumming wildly against her breasts. "I can't hold on much longer."

She didn't want him to hold on at all. How could he doubt she wanted him when she was lying against him as pliantly as putty? "Roman, you idiot. I *want* you."

His hips moved back and forth, thrusting and retreating in jerky rhythm to his words, filling her with hard pulsing desire. "Tell me what you want me to do to you. Do you like this?"

"Yes." Her hands ran up his shoulders, exploring the swell of muscles beneath his smooth, tanned skin. She instinctively widened her stance. "I think I . . ." She closed her eyes and her hands clenched on his shoulders as the muscles of her stomach knotted with painful tension. "Maybe not. I'm hurting so. . . ."

"Here?" His hand slid down beneath the layers of clothing to gently, sensuously rub the naked flesh of her stomach. He laughed softly as he felt her muscles contract beneath his hand. His hand wandered farther, and his palm cupped her, twining his thumb into the tight curls he found below. "And here?"

She swayed toward him with a little cry, jabs of lightning surging through her with every stroke of those long, clever fingers. Her eyes opened slowly, languorously, to see his face only inches from her own, his gaze intent, his lips curved with heavy sensuality.

"And what about here?"

She gasped and a shudder racked her body. His fingers . . . She stood there, immobile, staring into his eyes as if hypnotized. She couldn't have moved a muscle even if she'd been told a cyclone would strike the next moment. A cyclone would have been minor compared to the tempest her body was experiencing.

"Tell me what you want." His voice was as soft as velvet and was coaxing, wooing her. "Words excite you. Say those words, Manda."

"I want you . . . inside me." She had to wait a moment to recover from the wave of heat that rolled over her. He was right. Saying the words added to the excitement she was feeling. "I want your tongue on my breasts." The clenching in her stomach spasmed once more, and her breath was coming in little gasps. "Roman, I can't talk anymore. I can't—"

"Lord, neither can I!" His hands left her. An instant later the khaki shorts and the bikini panties beneath them were sliding to the floor. Then he lifted her up and carried her to the bedroom.

"My tennis shoes," she said vaguely. It seemed oddly undignified to be totally nude with the exception of her shoes.

"I'll take care of it," he said as he laid her on the deep brown satin coverlet. "I'll take care of everything."

He was already taking care of everything. The tennis shoes were gone, and he was stripping the rest of his own clothes off quickly. In the dusky half-light he appeared as a huge shadow standing over her. His broad shoulders tapered down to a slim waist and hips, and his heavily corded thighs bulged with brawny power. She suddenly felt very small and defenseless lying before him. Strange. She couldn't ever remember experiencing a feeling of helplessness before. Did all women feel this same sensation of weakness in the final moment before total physical commitment?

She was acutely conscious of even the most minute details of her surroundings. The drumming of the rain on the metal roof, the cool feel of silk beneath her naked body, the silver gleam of a mirror on the wall beyond Roman's shoulder.

"You're so little," he said. "I didn't realize how little you were until now." His tense voice echoed her reaction as if he had read her mind. "I know I'm a big man, and I'll do my best not to hurt you. Don't be afraid of me, Manda."

Warmth and tenderness banished her temporary uncertainty. She held out her arms. "I'm not afraid. I'll never be afraid of you." She laughed huskily. "I'm only afraid you won't *hurry.*"

She couldn't see his expression in the dimness of the room, but she knew he was smiling. There was a smile in his voice as he sat down on the bed beside her. "No chance of that. I couldn't slow down now even if you asked me to." His large hand hovered over her breast. "You have magnificent breasts. You should never wear anything to cover them. I'd like to keep you prisoner in a lovely suite where only I could come to see you. I'd dress you in silks and velvets, but they'd all be designed to reveal your wonderful breasts." His hand closed on her left breast.

She gasped. She'd been expecting it, but his warm hard hand still came as a sensual shock. He hesitated, and she could feel his gaze on her face. "I didn't hurt you?"

"No." His thumbnail was flipping back and forth

on her nipple, and she had to bite her lip to keep from moaning. "You have a very erotic imagination."

He slowly lowered his head. "You couldn't say the words, so I'm saying them for you. Do you think you'd like dressing like that for me? Can you see me coming into the room and moving toward you? I'd walk very quickly because all through the day I would have been thinking about you waiting for me. By the time I walked through the door, I'd be ready to explode." His lips brushed back and forth on her erect, pointed nipple. "Just as I am now." His tongue flicked out slowly, teasingly. "You're trembling. I'm trembling too, love. Does it excite you to know all you have to do is let me touch you, and I tremble?" He went on with his fantasy tale, interspersing it with strokes of his tongue and the gentle pressure of his teeth. "I'd try to spend a long time pleasuring your breasts because I love them so much, but I wouldn't be able to hold out for long. I'd pull you down to the soft white fur of the carpet and move over you." He was over her now, parting her thighs. "I'd be nearly frantic by that time, and I'd push up your silk skirt and . . ." His fingers were rubbing, stroking. She gasped, her hips arching helplessly up to him. "I hope I'd be able to wait until you were ready for me, but I don't know if I could be that patient. I'd be so wild for you. My guts would be tied in knots, and all I'd be able to think about is how wonderful it would be to come into you. To have you take every bit of me." He slid slowly between her thighs. She clenched her teeth and held her breath. Fullness. Heat.

He paused and was still. Great shudders racked his body. "End of fantasy," he said thickly. "The rest is reality. All right, Manda?"

She was breathing so hard her answer was almost a whisper. "All right."

"Will you take me?"

Didn't he know she wanted nothing else more passionately? "Yes." She moistened her lips. "Oh, yes."

He plunged forward. An instant of blinding pain caused her to cry out, then there was only hot fullness and savage satisfaction.

She felt him freeze above her. "Manda?"

"It's all right. I'm fine now." Her legs curled around his hips, and she hugged him to her. "I guess I was startled."

"You're not the only one." There was a touch of grimness in his tone. Another shiver ran through him. He flexed yearningly within her. "What the hell am I supposed to do now?"

"Go on." Her teeth pressed against his shoulder. She could barely speak. So full. Part of him. "For heaven's sake, go on."

"I don't think I have any choice." His voice was hoarse with desperation. "Lord, I can't even think."

She licked delicately at his shoulder. He tasted smooth and salty. "I like the way you taste too. Perhaps later . . ." She couldn't remember what she'd been about to say because he moved suddenly. Forceful, pistonlike strokes shook her to her foundations and drew low half-moans from deep inside her. Friction, beauty, a fiery hunger that fed and was reborn from its very satiation.

She could hear his harsh breathing somewhere above her. She wished she could see his face. He was deep, and then deeper inside her. She opened her lips in a silent scream to relieve the tension. Too much. Not enough. Pounding. Beauty. Heat. Her head tossed back and forth on the pillow. "Roman . . ." It was a whispered plea.

"Soon." The word was spoken through gritted teeth in a tone so guttural it was almost inaudible. "Move with me." His hands cupped her buttocks and lifted her into each stroke. "Give to me."

She gave to him in a flurry of response she thought would destroy her. The tension grew into a fever of hunger. The muscles of his thighs bulged, gripping her hips as his knees dug into the mattress. "More," he said thickly. "More, Manda."

There was no more. Only blinding rapture, a release from tension that offered not freedom, but a different bondage. Roman gave a low cry as he buried his lips in her throat.

It might have been minutes or hours before she was able to fight her way through the silken languor that was filling her senses. Her heart was still beating wildly and she felt too lazy even to open her eyes. She wanted to stay where she was forever. Possessed, possessing, fulfilled.

"I'm crushing you," Roman said jerkily. "Though I don't know why I'm worrying about that now. I must have almost torn you apart." His voice was heavy with self-disgust. "And I said I'd be careful with you. How badly did I hurt you?"

"Hardly at all after the first . . ." She opened her eyes. "And what pain there was, I invited." She smiled. "As I'll always invite you, Roman."

He moved off her and swung his legs to the floor. He sat on the side of the bed, his hands clenched into fists, his spine taut with strain. "Why, Manda?"

"Why was I a virgin?" She shrugged. "I don't kn—" She stopped. "Maybe I do know. I guess I always knew someday the great adventure would come my way. I've gone after every bit of excitement and adventure that ever came beckoning to me, but maybe it was all leading up to this. Why become jaded and risk not recognizing the real thing when it came along?"

"The real thing?"

"Love," she said simply.

He was silent for a moment, as if searching for words. "You really meant it when you said you were in love with me?"

"You still don't believe me?"

"I'm beginning to think you believe it." His words were halting.

"Of course I believe it. I was pretty skeptical myself at first, but I guess it has something to do with heredity."

"I beg your pardon?"

"My father told me the first time he saw my mother he knew he was in love with her. He was visiting a small vineyard in the south, and he fell like a ton of bricks." She searched and found his hand on the coverlet and squeezed it affectionately. "I suppose it runs in the family."

"I see."

She lifted his hand to her lips and pressed a kiss on his palm. "Do you think you've come to love me just a little? I don't want to rush you, but sometimes I get impatient."

His expression was undiscernible in the dimness as he moved his hand from her lips to brush a shining strand of hair away from her face. "Manda, I want to give you what you want but—"

"You're not ready. Shhh. It's all right. It will make the adventure all the more exciting if I have to work for it."

He chuckled. "Good Lord, nothing fazes you, does it? You're incredible, Manda Delaney."

"I'm glad you realize that fact at least. Now come back to bed and let's snuggle. I understand snuggling is an important part of après lovemaking and I intend to squeeze every bit of enjoyment I can out of it."

He laughed again and lay down beside her, drawing her into a loving embrace, his fingers soothingly rubbing her temple as she cuddled closer, nestling her cheek in the hollow of his shoulder. "I'll be glad to offer any assistance I can."

"This is nice, isn't it?" She sighed contentedly. "The rain, the warmth, and being together."

"Very nice."

The room was silent except for the sound of their breathing, and the rain, like pebbles on the roof.

"Roman?"

"Hmmm?"

"When we were first driving in the rain, you were as happy and excited as I was. I *knew* you were. I could feel it."

"Yes."

Her index finger absently twined around a springy curl on his chest. "But then you changed. You weren't the same. Why did you change?"

"I remembered who I was and forgot what I had been."

Her brow wrinkled in puzzlement. "What?"

His lips smoothed the lines from her forehead. "You're a very persuasive lady. All of a sudden I was the same Roman Gallagher who had traipsed all over the world and risked his neck at the drop of a hat. I was eight years younger and enjoying the hell out of it."

"But that's the way it should be," she said eagerly. "It can always be that way, Roman." She laughed softly. "Just keep me around, and I'll show you. We'll be so good together. We'll see so many wonderful—"

He shook his head. "No, Manda," he said gently. "Because I'm not that man anymore."

"Why? What happened?"

"I grew up."

She didn't speak for a long time. He would have thought she was asleep except for the restless movement of her finger on his chest. "It was so much fun." Her whisper was poignantly wistful. "I thought you understood."

"I do understand." His lips brushed her temple. "I understand the thrill and the search and the excitement. I understand all those wonderful things."

"But you gave them up."

"No, I didn't give them up. I just moved on."

"Roman, I . . ." Her voice trailed off. "I don't want to talk about it anymore." She planted a kiss on his shoulder and cuddled closer. "I'll convince you of the error of your ways some other time."

He felt a sudden pang of empathy. She was running away. But how far could she run before she came face-to-face with her nemesis? "Fine. I have other things I'd rather discuss anyway." His lips covered hers with a sweet, sensuous heat. "Wouldn't you like me to tell you another one of my fantasies? This time you're in a beautiful Persian garden, and all you have on is a . . ."

Five

He was aware of someone moving quietly, with the utmost care, in the bedroom.

Roman sleepily opened his eyes, realizing at once he was alone in bed. "Manda?"

"Go back to sleep." She bent down and gave him a swift kiss. "I was just leaving you a note."

"A note." He raised himself up on one elbow, narrowing his eyes to try to discern her face in the darkness. "Where the hell do you think you're going? Come back to bed."

"I can't. It's after ten o'clock."

"So? Do you turn into a pumpkin after ten? Even Cinderella could stay out until the last stroke of midnight."

She laughed softly and kissed him again. "Cinderella didn't have Jacto waiting for her. I don't want him to worry. I made a pot of espresso and filled a thermos to take to him. Would you like me to bring you a cup before I leave?"

He shook his head. "I don't want you to leave. I

want you to come back to bed. I'll send one of the crew to bring Jacto his damn coffee."

"I really have to go. It's stopped raining, and it's cooler out now. I have to take advantage of the break in the weather. I'll be able to work through the night." She straightened and turned away. "I'll see you tomorrow evening."

She was actually leaving him. Roman felt a rush of emotions, a mixture of anger and fear. "I'm sorry I didn't make your first experience enjoyable enough to make you want to spend the entire night with me."

"Oh, Roman . . ." She turned around and sat down on the bed. There had been an unmistakable thread of pain beneath the bitter mockery in his tone. "I didn't mean to hurt your feelings."

"You didn't hurt my feelings." He shrugged carelessly. "It was over. Why shouldn't you leave?"

"It's not over. It's just begun." She needed to see his face, dammit. She reached over and turned on the lamp on the bedside table, but the light was of little help. His expression was as impassive as his tone had been. "It will never be over. It's just that I have commitments right now. Don't you think I want to come back to bed?"

"I don't have any idea what you want to do." He was looking past her at the mirror on the far wall. "I have commitments too. I usually work until after midnight when I'm in the middle of a picture. Perhaps you're right, and we've both been neglecting our priorities. By all means, run along to your mysterious commitment."

"How can you act like this?" Manda sighed. "What can I say to make you understand?"

"I don't want to understand." His voice was suddenly rough. "I want you to come back to bed and stay here until morning. I want to make love to you again and again until—" He broke off. Until what? Until he had imprinted his mind and soul as well as his body on her? Until he had made sure he had forged a bond that would hold her until he wanted to let her go? What kind of selfish bastard was he anyway? he asked himself. He had refused to commit to anything beyond a sexual relationship, but he was still trying to put chains on Manda. He smiled with effort. "I told you I could be difficult. Go on. I'll see you tomorrow."

She rose slowly, still gazing at him with troubled eyes. "I wouldn't go if I didn't have to, Roman."

"I understand." He didn't understand, blast it. He wanted her to be willing to toss her precious plans over the moon in order to be with him. "Perhaps another time."

"Tomorrow." She smiled lovingly. "I promise, Roman." She turned and walked swiftly to the door. "I'll be here at sundown."

He nodded. "Tomorrow."

With one last smile and a wave she was gone.

A moment later he heard the heavy front door slam behind her. Silence. Loneliness. Both assaulted him with near-physical force. It was incredible how the absence of one woman could bring about a change in him.

No! He wouldn't let himself be affected like this. He wouldn't permit himself to be dependent on a Peter Pan who could say she loved him one minute and fly away the next. So what if she was everything he had ever dreamed a woman could be? He had always liked variety in bed, and would probably grow bored with her in a week or two.

Roman sat up and swung his feet to the floor. He stood and walked briskly toward the bathroom. He would shower, drink a cup of espresso, and then get to work making script changes for tomorrow's shooting. It wasn't as if a world-shaking event had occurred in his bed tonight. He had merely spent a pleasant few hours with . . .

Lord, he didn't want to feel frustration and turmoil.

He looked at his reflection in the mirror of the medicine cabinet, and his lips twisted in a sardonic smile. Why should she want to stay? He wasn't good-looking, had an awful temper, and had refused to offer her the comfort of the usual pretty promise of undying devotion. Next time he would try to be more civilized.

But he couldn't be civilized around Manda. He had proved that tonight. He could only walk the tightrope between the lust and the tenderness that she evoked so effortlessly in him. Tenderness. Somehow he had to rid himself of that response to her. Why did he have to understand her so very well? He could see in her everything he had been eight years ago. He even felt as if he could read her mind at times. But understanding led to tenderness which led to something infinitely more dangerous. So he would have to forget his feelings and concentrate on the purely physical emotions she ignited in him. It shouldn't be difficult. Just the memory of her caused an aching throb in his groin. He turned away from the mirror and smiled grimly. His shower would definitely have to be an ice-cold one.

The shower only served to wake him up and make him more conscious of the aching hunger he felt. Perhaps she wasn't Peter Pan after all, but Morgan

Le Fay. She sure as hell had worked a mystical spell on him, he realized. He shrugged on his terry-cloth robe and strode into the living room.

He sat down on the couch before the typewriter on the coffee table and inserted a sheet of paper. He firmly blocked all thoughts of cinnamon hair and bright amber eyes and began to type. He would work until he was tired enough to forget Manda and could go to sleep. Lord knows, the way he was feeling at the moment, he might not be tired for a number of hours, if at all. Even as he began to type, an errant thought slipped effortlessly through the wall he had erected in his mind to keep her out.

Tomorrow. He would see her tomorrow.

It was almost dark.

Roman took a drink of bourbon and stared broodingly through the window at the last scarlet streaks lighting the evening sky. He would give her another five minutes, and then he would go after her. She had promised, dammit. What kind of game did she think she was playing? Did she think she had him where she wanted him now that—

Someone knocked briskly on the door. It couldn't be Manda. Her knock was now only perfunctory before she opened the door and ran into the room.

"Come in."

Dennis Billet smiled genially as he came up the steps and into the room. "Some of the boys are getting together for a poker game in the mess tent. Want to sit in?"

"I'm going to be busy," Roman said curtly. "Maybe next time." He finished his bourbon in two swallows, got up, and crossed to the bar. "Have you seen Manda today?"

"Yep, right before she left this morning."

Roman's hand froze as he reached for the bottle of bourbon. "Left?"

Dennis nodded. "You didn't know?" A frown wrinkled his forehead. "Maybe I was supposed to tell you. She was in such a hurry, she was kind of confused. She and Jacto drove into Coober Pedy to catch a plane for Melbourne."

Roman kept his face expressionless.

"She received a call and said she had to go to Melbourne on personal family business."

"I see." Roman carefully finished pouring bourbon into his glass and put the cap on the bottle. "When will she be back?"

Dennis shrugged. "She didn't say. Knowing Manda, I'd say it could be a day or it could be a year."

It wasn't pain he was feeling, Roman assured himself. It was anger. She had left him without a word, and he was angry. He had a right to be angry. She had broken her promise.

He took a sip of bourbon, and it spread a comforting glow that dulled the—he blocked the thought quickly. It was natural to feel disappointed. She had been exceptionally good in bed, and he hadn't had his fill of her. Even now the muscles of his abdomen were knotted with hunger as he remembered how she felt under him as he moved. . . .

"Roman?"

He jerked his attention back to the man standing beside him. "What did you say? I was thinking of something else."

"I asked if you'd like to reconsider." Dennis's hazel eyes were twinkling. "I've got a real yen to take you to the cleaners. That engine overhaul cost me a mint."

"Not as much as the bet you placed on that nag at the Sydney handicap," Roman said absently. He finished his drink and set his glass down on the bar.

"What can I say?" Dennis asked. "Like any true Aussie, I place a bet now and then. There's nothing wrong with that."

"I guess not." Roman couldn't have cared less for Dennis's passion for the ponies at the moment. His hand suddenly closed on the neck of the bourbon bottle. "Sure, why not? There's bloody little else to do out here." He turned toward the door, taking the bourbon bottle with him. "Let's play poker."

"You drive on to the camp, Jacto," Manda said as she jumped out of the Jeep. "I just want to tell Roman I'm back. I shouldn't be more than thirty minutes."

Jacto nodded. "I will build the fire and start supper."

She waved and turned away, barely able to contain her eagerness. Her stomach was fluttering with excitement as she walked quickly to the door of the mobile home. It had seemed more like three years than three days since she had last seen Roman. Lord, she had missed him. She hadn't expected to be lonely. When she left someone she loved, she always felt sad, but it wasn't long until some fresh excitement diverted her. Not this time. Loneliness had been her painful and constant companion even while she had been with her dad and her sisters. At first, it had bewildered her, but gradually she had accepted it as part of the new and challenging experience of loving Roman.

She pounded cheerfully on the door, and then opened it and ran up the steps. "Roman, I'm back. Did you miss me? You'd better say yes because I . . ." Her words trailed off as a chill went through her.

Roman was sitting on the couch across the room, his fingers on the keyboard of the typewriter in front of him. He glanced up impassively before his gaze returned to the paper. He finished typing the sentence he had started. "You're a little late. I believe our date was for three days ago."

Her smile faded and then disappeared entirely. "You're angry with me."

"Now, why should I be angry? You're perfectly free to go where you please." He didn't look up. "It was a trifle rude of you not to leave a message but—"

"I did leave a message. I told Dennis to tell you I had a family emergency and had to go away for a few days. Didn't he let you know?"

"You evidently didn't take the time to make yourself clear. Did you ever hear of a pen and paper?"

"I was in such a hurry—" She stopped and then began again. "I'm sorry. I'd never have been discourteous if I'd realized—"

"Discourteous!" His eyes blazed as he lifted his gaze from the page. A shock ran through her. "Lord, what an anemic word. Three nights ago you were in my bed, and now you sound as regretful as if you'd chosen the wrong fork for the salad."

Manda felt a flare of answering anger. "I said I was sorry. What else do you want me to do? Maybe I should have made myself clearer, but there's nothing I can do about that now. Do you want me to go down on my knees and beg your forgiveness?"

He stood up and came toward her. "The thought has possibilities. I'd enjoy the hell out of having you on your knees." His black eyes were glittering in his taut face, and a muscle was jerking in his cheek. "I don't like what you've been doing to me, Manda."

"I haven't done anything to you. You act as if I'm some kind of vamp!" Suddenly the anger drained from her and only disappointment and weariness remained. "I don't want to argue any longer." She turned to the door. "I'll see you tomorrow, Roman."

"The hell you will." His hand spun her around to face him. "You said that three nights ago. I'm not letting you leave again."

"Roman, I—"

Her words were lost as his mouth crushed down on hers. She couldn't breathe. She could feel his teeth pressed painfully against her lower lip. She tried to move her head, but his fingers were tangled in her hair, his hands holding her still as his lips and teeth bruised her mouth.

He lifted his head. "Do you know what you're doing to me? I can't sleep, I can't work, I can't—" He broke off, his gaze on her lower lip. "Oh, God." His expression was no longer angry, but sick. "You're bleeding. I hurt you," he said dully.

His hands fell away from her hair and he stepped back. "Stay right there." He turned and strode into the bathroom. He immediately returned carrying a damp washcloth. He gently dabbed at her lower lip. He looked pale in spite of his tan. "I told you to go away. I told you I'd hurt you."

"It doesn't hurt now." Strangely enough, she felt no trace of anger or fear. She felt only a poignant sense of empathy and intense pity. She couldn't stand to see the pain and self-disgust on Roman's face. She wanted to do something, anything, to banish his hurt. "You scarcely broke the skin. You didn't mean to hurt me."

"Are you making excuses for me?" His lips twisted. "Stick around. If I didn't hurt you tonight, I probably would have the next time." He threw the washcloth on the bar. "Get the hell out of here."

She hesitated, her troubled gaze fixed on him. "No, not yet. Not until you tell me why. It wasn't just my leaving you without writing a note, was it?"

He shook his head, not looking at her. "No." His gaze returned to her face, and she inhaled sharply as she saw the torment there. "I missed you," he said simply. "I nearly went crazy while you were gone. I kept thinking of how hot and sweet you were the other night in bed, and I ached. . . . But that's not all. I kept remembering little things about you. How you laugh, how your eyes light up when you're excited, how you make every moment special."

Her eyes were beginning to glow, and a radiant smile illuminated her face. "I've got you, haven't I? You have to love me a little bit or you wouldn't have missed me so much."

"Are you crazy? Doesn't it mean anything to you that I've just acted like a barbaric madman? I *hurt* you, dammit. What are you, some kind of masochist?"

"No." She knew there was nothing barbaric about Roman. Why couldn't he realize his very self-castigation was evidence of that fact? However, she could see there would be no convincing him at the moment. She grinned. "But I don't see why I should tongue-lash you when you're doing such a good job on yourself." Taking a step closer, she reached up to caress his cheek gently.

"No!" He flinched. "Don't touch me."

Her hand fell away. "But I want to touch you. I want to be close to you. Don't shut me out."

He closed his eyes. "Please go away, Manda. I can't take much more."

"I only want to help you."

"I know." There was a touch of wonder in his voice. "I don't understand why, yet I know you do. But you can't help me now." He opened his eyes. "I'm exposed . . . naked. I've never been more vulnerable in my life and I have to come to terms with it."

Her brow knotted in a frown. "You really want me to leave?"

"Please."

She looked at him, her teeth nibbling at her lower lip. "Sure?"

"Sure."

"All right, but I'll be back tomorrow. You won't get rid of me easily." She turned to the door and then glanced over her shoulder and smiled tentatively. "I *have* got you. Right?"

His answering smile was both weary and sad. "Oh, yes, you've definitely got me."

Her smile widened happily. "Wonderful!" She opened the door. "I'll see you later."

He nodded. "Later." Then, as she started to go down the steps, he called her name.

She spun around to face him.

"Your family emergency." His words were halting, jerky. "I hope nothing is wrong."

She nodded. "Everything's under control. It just took a bit of doing. Good night, Roman."

He watched the door shut behind her, and the tension flowed out of his muscles. It had been damn close. All he would have had to do was to reach out and take what he wanted. She gave of herself so naturally that she wouldn't have thought of holding back, but he couldn't take from her tonight. Instead, he had to think about giving, and it wasn't going to be easy after all the years of living within and for himself. He realized that the night ahead was going to be even more torturous than the three that had gone before.

Six

"Manda."

She stirred, easing from sleep to half waking. Then her eyes suddenly flicked open. "Roman?"

He was bending over her bedroll, his features shadowed and indistinct in the gray light of predawn. "Come with me."

She sat up and glanced across the campfire at Jacto, wrapped in his blanket. He appeared to be sound asleep, but that didn't mean he was. She hurriedly slipped on her tennis shoes and ran her fingers through her tousled hair before rising to her feet and following Roman silently from the camp.

"Where are we going?" she asked when they had covered several yards. "Back to your trailer?"

"No, I want to show you something." He was moving swiftly, and she had to hurry to keep pace with him.

"You could have waited while I changed." She glanced down at her white shorts and matching tank top. "I feel rumpled."

"You're beautiful." He wasn't looking at her, but there was no doubting the sincerity in his voice. "You're always beautiful." They reached his Jeep parked at the perimeter of the opal field. "Get in. We aren't going far."

The Jeep was in motion almost before she settled onto the passenger seat.

The morning breeze was cool on her face and she felt a tingle of excitement as she remembered their previous trip into the desert. She glanced at him. There was something different about him, something new.

He looked the same as always. He was wearing close-fitting beige jeans, and the short sleeves of his army-green bush jacket revealed the brawny muscles of his upper arms. His big hands on the steering wheel were deft and controlled and she found her memory wandering to the way those hands made her feel.

He turned toward her. "Did you say something?"

She hadn't been aware of uttering a sound, but her breathing had unconsciously quickened and that must have been what he had heard. "No," she said quickly. "Are we almost there?"

"Yes, right around the other side of the ridge." His gaze lifted to the horizon, which was now streaked with pink and gold. "And just in time."

"You're being very mysterious. What is all of this— Dear heaven." The vision before her was dazzling. "It's incredible."

"Yes." He had stopped the Jeep and was leaning his arms across the steering wheel. "I ran across it yesterday. I was going to use it as a setting for a scene in the picture." He paused. "But last night I changed my mind and decided I'd give it to you instead. Do you like it, Manda?"

"Like it? It's glorious!"

Standing on a slight incline was a massive wall of slate-gray rock cleaved in the center as if by a blow from Vulcan's hammer. It looked as if it had stood on this spot since the beginning of dreamtime and would remain throughout eternity. The rock was impregnated by a wild array of minerals, streaking its slate-darkness with orange, ochre, emerald, and amethyst.

The first rays of dawn hit the rock and Manda gave a cry of delight. The boulder also contained tiny quartz crystals which caused it to glitter in the sunlight and set all the colors aflame. "I've never seen anything so beautiful." Then she noticed something else, another miracle, stretching from the incline on which the rock stood into the distance. "Flowers!"

She jumped out of the Jeep and ran toward the oasis of brilliant color and heady scent that lay before her. Wild flowers were everywhere, carpeting the rust-brown of the sandy desert floor with exquisite beauty.

Golden-hearted daisies in delicate shades of pink, pale lavender, and pristine white tumbled over the landscape. A crystal-clear creek bubbled and twisted through the magical natural garden, nurturing its beauty. Surrounded only by flat brown desolation, this small haven of beauty shimmered radiantly in contrast. "How could it happen? In the middle of the desert . . . It's a miracle."

"Yes, but a very natural one. Millions of seeds buried deep in the earth, just waiting for a touch to bring them to life."

"The storm."

He nodded. "The storm." He walked slowly toward her. "Since we've met, I've never given you anything. I've only taken. I think perhaps I had forgotten how to give." He stopped before her. "This is my first gift, Manda."

She smiled shakily. "You certainly start off with a bang."

"I hurt you." A shadow crossed his face. "I know this doesn't make up for what I did, but maybe you can throw it on the balance scales and let me build on it."

"Oh, Roman . . ." She loved him so much she felt as if she were going to splinter into a zillion shining pieces at any moment. She turned into his arms and nestled close to him. "You don't have to build. You're *there.*"

"No." His hands touched her shoulders lightly, almost tentatively. "I've got a long way to go, but maybe it's a start. I did a lot of thinking last night and made a few decisions. One of them is that I have to accept what's happened to me." He pushed her away and looked down at her. "I love you, Manda Delaney. I think I'm going to love you for the rest of my life."

Manda felt a wild heady surge of pure joy. "I love you too," she whispered. "I love you so much, Roman."

He slowly shook his head. "You don't love me. Right now you're only in love with the grand adventure of falling in love, but maybe I can build on that too. I hope to hell I can."

"No, I really do—"

His fingers covered her lips. "Shhh, it's all right. It will come. It only takes time and growing."

"But you're wrong. I do love you. I—"

"Do you want to marry me, Manda?"

Her eyes widened in surprise. "I never thought about it."

His lips twisted. "I didn't think you had. Did you think about having my children and staying with me through sickness and health? Did you think about sharing dreams and then turning those dreams into reality?"

She was gazing at him uncertainly. "This is all new to me. Give me a little time."

"I didn't need time. I knew as soon as I realized I loved you that I wanted all those things." His fingers moved from her lips to stroke her cheek. "But I'll give you all the time you need. I have a few things I have to work on too. I'm not big on trust and you've already seen I have the devil of a temper." He kissed her gently. "Just don't run away from me. I'll find a way of dealing with it. I can deal with anything as long as you stick around."

"I'll stick around," she promised. Her voice was husky, but her sudden smile was radiant. "You couldn't drive me away." She grabbed his hand. "Come on. Let's walk among the flowers. I want to touch them, smell them." She pulled him into the field of velvet-petaled blossoms. "Who knows if they'll be here tomorrow?"

Like Manda, Roman thought, experiencing a sharp twinge of pain. But Manda *would* be here tomorrow, and, if she weren't, he would find a way of accompanying her wherever she wandered. He wasn't going to lose her now. His hand tightened around hers. "The flowers will still be here. They just might be hiding in the earth again. Waiting." He smiled gently. "But someday the waiting will be over and they'll bloom again."

"But *I* don't want to wait. They're so beautiful right now, like a magical island in a sea of—" She suddenly chuckled with delight. "An island. I've at last found my magical island."

"Island?"

She nodded, her amber eyes twinkling. "When I was seven, I decided what I wanted to do most in the world was build a raft and sail down the Murray River to the sea. But I didn't want to go alone, so I talked Addie and Sydney into going with me. It wasn't easy. They were both older than I was and a heck of a lot more practical."

"But you did it?"

"Oh, yes, I did it. I concocted this wonderful story of a mysterious island lying just south of Australia. It was an island carpeted with exotic flowers, where all sorts of magical things could happen." Manda's laughter had faded and her eyes were misty and faraway. "An island where the dreamtime still existed, where every day would be a new adventure and we would all have whatever we wanted. A golden-horned unicorn for Addie and black swans flying for Sydney and . . ." She shook her head as if to clear it. "I don't think Sydney and Addie really believed me, but they let me talk them into it anyway."

"Perhaps they wanted to believe. It's not often children are offered the possibility of having their dreams fulfilled. You gave them that."

"Not for very long. The raft struck a sandbar and my father found us before we could push it off again." She grimaced. "We'd been gone more than twenty-four hours and Dad had rounded up all the neighbors to search for us. He definitely wasn't pleased."

"I can imagine. Were you punished?"

She nodded. "You bet we were. He tanned us good and proper."

A faint smile touched his lips. "Somehow I can't believe that would have discouraged you. Did you try again?"

"No." There was a flicker of regret in her voice. "I couldn't convince Sydney and Addie to go with me. The adventure was over for them and I didn't want to go alone."

"No, you told me you don't like to be alone."

"I wish I had known you then, Roman. You would have gone with me, wouldn't you?"

"I would have gone with you."

"And we would have reached the sea?"

"Yes." Roman's voice was very soft. "And we would have found your island of dreams, Manda. Unicorns and black swans flying and adventure every day. I would have given them all to you."

She turned to face him, her face alight with joy. "And you say I don't love you. How could I not love a man who would give me all that?"

Sunrise was tangling in her hair and turning it into a golden halo. He suddenly wanted to thread his fingers in that silken fire and forget everything except how much he wanted her. As she had said, if flowers are blooming, why not enjoy them? Eight years ago he would have had no qualms about living for the moment.

But he wasn't that man any longer, and one Peter Pan in a relationship was more than enough. He lifted her hand and pressed a light kiss on the palm. "I have every intention of making quite sure you find me irresistible and I'll not have even the slightest hesitation about using any bribery necessary."

Manda experienced a ripple of uneasy concern.

There was something very wrong with what he had just said. Something she should try to make right. Then she instinctively pushed the thought away. Later. She would worry about it later. Now the sun was shining, and the flowers were giving off a scent that was dizzily intoxicating, and she was with Roman. Nothing could be too wrong in a world like this.

She sank down among the daisies and pulled him down beside her. "Talk to me. I've told you all about my childhood misdemeanors. It's only fair that you reciprocate. Were you a hell-raiser too?"

"No." He looked out over the field of flowers. "I was a very well-behaved child." His lips twisted. "I know that may be hard for you to believe, considering what a bad-tempered bastard the final product has turned out to be."

She grinned. "Let's just say I can't imagine you as the model child."

"Oh, I wasn't a model child by any means." His words were laced with bitter irony. "I didn't even come close. No matter how hard I tried, I never reached beyond the first level of the pyramid. I was a complete disappointment to my mother."

"No one could expect a child to be perfect. Lord knows my father would have been sadly disillusioned if he'd had any hopes about that." Her smile disappeared. "You have to be mistaken. Parents may have high hopes for their children, but they come to understand our shortcomings as well as our strengths."

"I understand some parents do. That wasn't my experience." He shrugged. "I'm not condemning my mother. I even came to understand her after a while. She was one of those people who couldn't bear to have anything ugly or inferior around them.

I often thought she must have divorced my father because she found marriage to be inexcusably flawed. You see, she was a collector of beautiful things. She owned an art gallery in Perth and was very discriminating about the items she accepted. It wasn't reasonable she would accept anything less than perfect in her personal life."

"Reasonable?" Manda echoed. "Reason has nothing to do with the love between parent and child."

"It doesn't, does it?" His lips curved in a bittersweet smile. "It took me a long time to understand that particular truth. I never realized I had a right to love. I always thought it was something I had to earn by being the smartest, the most accomplished, the best behaved. . . . I knew I couldn't hope to be anything but physically unappealing to her, but I thought I might make up for it if I worked hard enough."

Manda felt her throat tighten painfully. "And did you?"

"No." His gaze left the desolation of the desert and met her eyes. "I never stood a chance." His hand reached out to touch the scar on his cheek. "And then I came back from 'Nam with this. I visited her once when I first came back to Perth. I sat in her perfect living room, in her perfect house and had tea from her perfect Wedgwood tea service. She was polite, but she didn't look at my face. Not once. I never went back."

"Oh, God," Manda whispered. There was so much pain beneath Roman's calm surface. "I'm sorry, Roman." Her tone was suddenly fierce. "She was a stupid woman. Didn't she realize how special you were? You're brilliant and sensitive and—"

"Hold it!" He chuckled. "I didn't tell you my life's

story to make you pity me. All that was a long time ago."

Yet the scars were still deeper and more sensitive than the one on his cheek. "I want to *strangle* her."

He shook his head. "It wasn't her fault, it was mine. You can't change people's basic nature. I was just too stubborn to accept it. I had to learn from experience." He smiled. "But I like the fact you're being so defensive. It . . . warms me."

She could feel the tears brimming and blinked rapidly to keep them back. She wanted to warm him and hold him and keep him from all pain. The maternal strength of the emotion astonished her. She had never been a caretaker, but with passionate intensity she wanted to take care of Roman.

He suddenly frowned. "Hey." His index finger gently touched her wet lash. "I told you I didn't want pity. The only reason I told you about my childhood was that I felt I owed it to you." He grinned. "Call it another gift. I guarantee it's a very rare one. I've never stripped myself naked for anyone before. It feels a little drafty."

"Roman, I—"

"No, forget it." He stood up and reached down to pull her to her feet. "Come on, it's time we went back to the encampment. I have to shoot two scenes with those blasted camels today, and I'll be lucky if I have them in the can by sundown. Damn, I've never seen a more stubborn, foul-tempered creature." He chuckled. "Except when I look in the mirror."

Manda was silent and unusually subdued as they walked slowly back to the Jeep.

"Something wrong?" Roman asked.

"No. Everything's fine." She got into the passenger seat, her gaze wandering to the sweeping glory of the wild flowers. Roman's gift to her. He had given her other gifts today as well, and each one was as precious as this beautiful panorama before her. Yet she was experiencing a curious discontent. She had taken his gifts and returned nothing. She had always been heedless, a little careless, but now she was troubled by that aspect of her character. Oh, well, there would be another time. She turned to him and smiled. "I was just thinking what a very lucky lady I am."

"Dammit, Roman, I won't work with them." Brent's voice was muffled, but his irritation came through loud and clear as he pressed the ice bag on his swollen nose with extreme care. "I've put up with heat, boredom, and celibacy for this picture, but you can forget about those camels. I'll be lucky if I don't have to have rhino surgery before this is through and— Stop that chortling, blast it!"

Roman tried valiantly. "Sorry," he said solemnly as he sat down on the couch. "I realize what a traumatic experience you've gone through, but look at it this way: That was a female camel and she was probably only giving you a little love nip. You know how devastating you are to the female of any species."

"Nip?" Brent asked indignantly. "That bitch tried to bite off my nose. And yesterday her male counterpart threw me onto my rump. I suppose you're going to tell me he was trying to express his affection too."

"Well, I'm not sure." Roman tilted his head as if considering. "Is there such a thing as a gay camel?"

"Roman, damn you, this is serious."

"I'll have to take a look at your contract. Now we know it covers falling off the edge of the world and dust asphyxiation, but I'm not sure you're covered for attacks by lovesick camels."

Brent lifted the ice bag long enough to take a deep breath and glare at Roman. "I think I'm going to murder you. What have I got to lose? I'd have no problem proving justifiable homicide."

"I wouldn't try it. I might have to sic my camels on you."

"You won't think it's so funny when you have to shoot around me for the next four days."

"It will be worth it." Roman could no longer suppress a grin. "I don't think I've laughed so hard in the last ten years. And I believe I've just had a stroke of genius. The next picture I'll do will be the Jimmy Durante story and I'll cast you as the Schnoz. Of course, you may have some competition with old ski-nose, Bob Hope. I guess I'll just have to keep a camel around to bite—"

"Definitely justifiable homicide," Brent pronounced as he put the ice bag back on his nose. "You're mellow today. I think I preferred your Mr. Hyde persona. At least I wouldn't have had to contend with your flippant attitude toward this assault on my manly beauty."

Roman looked at him in surprise. He hadn't thought there had been any noticeable change in his demeanor, but evidently Brent was more perceptive than he'd believed. He couldn't say he'd felt exactly "mellow," particularly with the exasperation of working with the camels, but he had felt more serene than usual. Perhaps opening up his past and his emotions to Manda had acted as a catharsis to clear away years of corroding bitterness. "We have one more day of shooting with the camels, but maybe we can put a muzzle on them. I'll talk to the trainer."

"You're too kind," Brent said gloomily. "With my luck, there'll probably be some law forbidding muzzles on the grounds of cruelty to animals."

There was a brisk knock at the door. Roman was given no opportunity to answer before the door opened to reveal Dennis standing on the steps.

"Roman, I thought you'd want to see this," Dennis said as he came into the trailer. He tossed a folded newspaper onto the coffee table. "It was in the mailbag I brought from Sydney this morning. You're not going to like it."

"Good," Brent said. "He deserves a little unpleasantness after his callous disregard for my personal tragedy."

Dennis grinned. "I heard about your little accident. Nasty devils, aren't they? Serves you right, mate. If you remember, you tried to wish them on me and my Cessna."

"That was a joke. However, if you don't get that grin off your face, I may give up my percentage at the box office to persuade Roman to make you fly them *back* to Sydney. I'm beginning to relish the thought of that humpbacked cannibal nibbling on your ear while you're trying to land your precious Cessna. I can see you—" Brent broke off as Roman began to swear vehemently. The newspaper was spread out before Roman and his gaze was on a collection of pictures on the front page of the feature section. "I gather Dennis is right. You're not pleased. What's the problem?"

With scarcely restrained violence, Roman tossed the paper to him. "*This* is the problem. How the hell did they manage to get their paws on these pictures?"

Brent glanced down at the newspaper and gave a low whistle of surprise. "Candids. They've got shots of all of us. Even those damn camels." He frowned. "As a matter of fact, this close-up of that bloody camel is better than the one of me. Wouldn't you know she would upstage me?" He read the headline. "Exclusive pictures of Roman Gallagher's new blockbuster." He looked up. "You didn't give permission for this release?"

"Hell no! I told you I never permit newspaper stories while I'm filming."

"Which is why a picture feature like this is a marketable commodity," Dennis interjected. "Whoever sold you out must have made a bundle."

Brent's brow creased in a thoughtful frown. "You think one of the crew decided to line his pockets on the side?"

"Who else?" Roman asked grimly. "It's not as if we have a stream of visitors coming and going."

"That's right." Brent slowly folded the paper. "But how would he have gotten the film out of Deadman's Ridge? The mailbag?"

"Do you think he would have taken the chance of sending a story to one of the largest newspapers in Australia in the company mailbag?" Dennis shook his head doubtfully. "Not likely. But damned if I know how else he could have done it. The only ones who have left Deadman's Ridge since you started shooting are me and Manda. I guess it had to be the mailbag."

Manda.

Roman felt an icy chill extinguish his anger. Manda had been a reporter at one time; Manda had said she had gone to Melbourne three days ago. Melbourne or Sydney? Manda had said Killaroo was in New South Wales. Why would a family emergency take her to Melbourne, which was in Victoria? "When did the story break?" he asked slowly.

Brent looked down at the paper. "Day before yesterday."

The chill deepened. It was logical, the pieces fit together.

"Do you want me to fly into Sydney and bring some security boys back to check into it?" Dennis asked.

Roman didn't answer.

"Roman?"

"What?" Roman shook his head. "No, not yet. It may be only a one-time occurrence. I don't want to start any trouble with the crew if it isn't necessary. We'll just keep an eye on what goes into the next mailbag." He stood up and strode to the door. "I think I'll go for a walk. I need to do some thinking."

Dennis frowned. "Are you sure? Security should really be notifi—"

"I said no!" Roman's words slashed out. "Not yet."

Dennis held up his hands in mock surrender. "Okay. Whatever you say. I didn't mean to challenge your authority."

Roman opened the door. "Sorry. I guess I'm a little on edge. I'll see you both later."

"Two visits to our humble camp in one day." Manda smiled warmly as she crossed the yards that separated the mine opening and the lean-to. "I was coming to see you, but I wanted to bathe in the billabong first." She ran her fingers through her dust-impregnated hair and made a face. "I'm positively filthy. Now that you're here though, I want you to meet

Jacto." She looked around and frowned. "Now, where the devil is he?"

"He took off when he saw me coming across the field. Evidently he doesn't want to make my acquaintance."

"Darn it. Jacto is acting very strange lately." She shrugged. "Oh, well, he'll let me know what it's all about eventually."

"Manda, what are you doing here?" Roman's question was harshly abrupt.

Manda's smile faded. "You know I can't tell you yet. You'll just have to trust me a little longer."

"I'm not big on trust, remember?" His lips tightened. "But I'm trying, dammit. Is what you're doing illegal?"

"What would you do if I said yes?" she asked curiously.

"Get you a lawyer and then spank your fanny until you couldn't sit down for a month."

She laughed. "It's not a illegal, but I appreciate the fact you wouldn't turn me over to the gendarmes."

He slowly shook his head. "No, I'd never do that. No matter what you did."

"You're acting as strangely as Jacto. Is something wrong?"

"No." He was still looking at her with painful intensity. "Manda, you know if you need money, you can come to me. I'll give you anything you want."

Five hundred thousand dollars? she wondered ruefully. He didn't realize what he was saying. There was no way she could ask him for that kind of money. "I appreciate your offer, but I like earning my own way. I'll let you know if I change my mind."

"Do that. Manda, I—" He stopped, as if searching for words.

Manda was looking at him in bewilderment. "Yes?"

"Nothing," he muttered as he turned away. "I'm going back to the trailer. Come as soon as you can."

She grinned. "Come running?"

The glance he threw over his shoulder caused her smile to vanish. There was desperation, anger, desire, and something else that shocked her. Fear. "Yes," he said tightly. "Come running."

Seven

"Look, are you going to tell me what the devil is going on?" Manda put her wineglass on the end table beside the couch. "I'm too tired to play guessing games tonight. All through dinner you've been as moody and unsociable as a eucalyptus-starved koala, and I've had enough."

"Why should anything be wrong?"

"How should I know?" she said between her teeth. "This morning everything was beautiful, and tonight you're treating me as if I were some kind of a criminal."

"Perhaps you're being oversensitive. Is there any reason why I should treat you as a criminal?" He looked down into the clear depths of the Chablis in his glass. "I told you I could be difficult. You'll find I'm a hell of a lot easier if people are honest with me."

"Are you still harping on the opal mine? You know I'll tell you what I'm doing there as soon as possible, dammit. I want to be open with you. It's just "

"No qualifications!" His voice was harsh with near violence. "No ifs or justs! I can take that from other people, but not from you. Do you know how many times I've been lied to in my life? When I was a kid, it was supposedly done for kindness' sake. 'Your mother was too busy to come to your graduation exercises.' 'You're not really ugly, but interesting-looking.' Then, later, the lies had nothing to do with kindness, only greed." He downed the wine in one swallow and placed the glass on the end table beside her own. "I'm trying to accept your secret, but it's not a simple thing for me to do. I'm feeling raw and used and I can be very . . . savage when I'm feeling like this."

"My God, I think you're threatening me." She was staring at him in disbelief.

"I'm not threatening you," he said wearily. "I'm trying to warn you."

"Warn me? Warn me against what?"

"Let's drop it. I don't want to talk anymore." He stood up and reached down to bring her to her feet. "There's one sure way I know we can communicate." He strode swiftly to the bedroom, pulling her behind him. "Let's go to bed."

"Roman, stop." Manda could feel her exasperation and frustration rising in equal proportions. "I don't *want* this, dammit."

"You will. You're a very hot lady." He flicked on the lamp and pushed her to a sitting position on the brown silk coverlet on the bed. His fingers were quickly unbuttoning his shirt. "You know you'll enjoy it once you relax."

"Relax and enjoy?" she asked. "I'll be damned if I'll relax."

He shrugged out of his shirt and threw it aside.

His muscles gleamed in the lamplight, and she was suddenly conscious of the strength of those muscles. She inhaled sharply and felt a stirring in the pit of her stomach. It seemed like a long time since he had made love to her, an impossibly long time. The sexual tension was abruptly swirling in charged waves around them.

"We'll see," he said. "Perhaps it would be more enjoyable for both of us if you didn't relax. You needn't look at me as if I'm some kind of rapist. I'm not about to force you, Manda." He began unbuttoning her sleeveless blouse. "Anytime you want me to stop, I will." He thrust the blouse open and unfastened her bra. He held her gaze as he slowly slipped the straps from her shoulders and then slid them down her arms until the garment dropped to the floor. "All you have to do is say the word." His palms cupped her breasts, gently weighing her heaviness, his hands opening and closing with a rhythmic pressure. She inhaled sharply as an aching tingle of desire surged through her. The pressure of his large hands was unbelievably erotic. His thumbs were flicking the crests of her nipples and his eyes holding her own were dark and smoky with hunger. "But why should you tell me no?" he asked softly. "You want this as much as I do, don't you?"

"Yes," she whispered. "But not like this, not—" She broke off with a little cry as his thumbs and forefingers closed on her nipples with just enough pressure to send a jolt of electricity through every vein in her body. The muscles of her belly clenched and released.

His gaze was narrowed and intent. "You like that?" He tugged gently and she gasped and closed her eyes, her spine arching as she swayed toward him.

"I do too. You're so damn lovely. Do you know how swollen and ripe you are? How hard and pointed your nipples are between my fingers?" His thumbs and forefingers were rubbing with gentle friction back and forth. "When you were gone, I lay in this bed and thought about you until I nearly went crazy. I hurt so. Just like I'm hurting now. Are you so hungry for me that you hurt like that, Manda?" His hand left her breast and slid slowly down her smooth abdomen. She shuddered. His palm was heavy and hard and left a trail of fire in its wake. "Open your eyes, love. I want to see how much you want me."

She opened her eyes. His expression was no longer hard or reckless. His lips held a heavy sensuality and his eyes were blazing. She could see the erratic throb of the pulse in his throat. "Tell me you want me," he said hoarsely. "I have to know that wasn't a lie too. You don't have to tell me you love me, but I have to know you want me."

"I do want you." Her words were halting, spoken through a haze of desire and bewilderment. "And I do love you."

He didn't answer as his fingers undid the snap of her cut-off jeans and he slowly slid them over her hips. "And what do you want me to do to you tonight?" He sank to his knees on the floor, his arms wrapping and enfolding her thighs and knees. The springy triangle of dark hair on his chest was a provocative abrasion against her thighs as his teeth nibbled at the soft flesh of her belly. "Do you like to see me kneeling here before you? Does it make you feel powerful? Would you like me to make up a fantasy about an Amazon who uses men and then discards them?" His palm was rubbing back and forth across the tight curls that guarded her womanhood.

He looked up and met her gaze as he plucked teasingly. "You're trembling. Perhaps you do like this." He blew gently and she made a hoarse, broken sound deep in her throat. His palms slid around to cup her buttocks and he began to squeeze gently. "We've only just begun to tap the reservoir of our fantasies, but you'll have to tell me what you like. Does power turn you on?"

She was swaying and his words came hazily through the sensual web he was weaving around her. *He* was turning her on. Every touch, the scent of him, the masculine aggressiveness of his big body. But there was something wrong, an edge beneath that rampant sensuality. What had he said? Power? She shook her head as much to clear it as in negation. "No, I've never wanted power over anyone."

"You prefer submission? I admit I like that game better myself." He was suddenly rising. "Just sit there and wait for me." He smiled. "I won't be long." He was stripping quickly.

She found herself sitting on the edge of the bed watching him. The brown satin coverlet was cool against her naked thighs. She needed that coolness, she was burning up and yet shivers of sensation were convulsing her. He was so big he dominated the small room and there was an element of danger in him tonight that excited even as it puzzled her.

He was naked and was again smiling at her with that odd gleam of recklessness in his eyes. He sat down on the bed beside her, careful not to touch her. "You're mine," he said softly. "I'm the commanding general of Caesar's invading forces in Britain and you're the daughter of a Saxon king. Your people are defeated and you're my captive. I saw you, wanted you, and told my men to bring you to my tent." He was still not touching her, but his gaze was running over her with tactile sensuality. "I've told you I'll free your father and work with your people to make the defeat easier." One hand reached out to finger the silky hair at her temple. "But only if you obey me, if you give me pleasure, if you become my mistress and my slave. You have no choice." His hand wandered down from her hair to cover her right breast. "Do you?"

His palm was heavy, burning her, stopping her breath. "No," she whispered. The excitement was unbearable, the imagery, Roman, his touch, his voice. "I don't think I do."

"Then come here." He sat there, his muscles coiled with tension as he spread his thighs, waiting. "Get up and stand before me. I wish you to pleasure me."

She didn't know if she could stand up. Her knees had no more consistency than water. Yet she found herself on her feet standing between his knees.

"That's right," he murmured. His lips suckled delicately at one pointed nipple. "Just stand there and let me take you with my mouth and my hands." His palms were running over her naked spine and down to the swell of her buttocks. He closed his eyes and a shudder ran through him. "I love the scent of you. You smell of flowers, and life, and woman. Sometimes all you have to do is pass within two feet of me and I become so aroused I'm aching with it."

The fantasy was becoming merged and absorbed in their own hunger for each other and she found that was even more exciting. "Roman, I don't think I can stand here any longer."

"Then sit." She was suddenly on his lap straddling him, his bold arousal cradled against her. "Take me. Pleasure me. Slowly."

She sagged against him, her breasts were lifting and falling with every breath. "It's too . . . much."

He misunderstood. His heavy lids lifted and she experienced a shock of sensation—desire as stark and primitive as the fantasy he had created for her. "No, you'll find it just enough," he said thickly. "Remember? You took me very well the last time. We fit. Bodies, minds, hearts. Come." His hands were cupping her, inching her slowly forward, filling her. His gaze was on the leaping pulse in the hollow of her throat and his nostrils were flaring. "You belong to me. You'll always belong to me. You *want* me here inside you, don't you?"

"Yes."

He brought her a little farther. Heat. An iron brand of possession. "Anytime I want you, you'll come. You'll give me your lips and your tongue and your breasts. You'll let me pull you down like this and come into you." He suddenly jerked her forward.

She gasped and clutched desperately at his shoulders. Unbearable fullness, total absorption. She clenched helplessly in an agony of satisfaction that was only a prelude of what was to come.

"Promise me."

She couldn't speak, she couldn't even think. She moved yearningly against him.

He was still holding her in that unbelievable captivity of intimacy. "Promise me."

"I promise." Her words were almost inaudible, forced from a throat too tight to speak.

"Good." There was a note of savage satisfaction in the word. "And I'll promise I'll always give you this." He fell back on the bed, taking her with him. He exploded, plunging, driving in a mindless rhythm of primitive desire.

She couldn't breathe, she couldn't move, she could only take and try to retain some semblance of sanity in the whirling passion enveloping them both. Then sanity was gone, and she didn't miss it. There was only Roman and possession and a splendor of togetherness. Her fingernails dug into his shoulders as she tried to stifle the moan welling in her throat.

"You want me." His eyes were blazing down at her in fierce triumph. "And that's no lie, is it?"

Lie? What was he saying? Nothing could be more basic or beautifully honest than this.

"Is it?" he demanded.

"I don't know what . . ." Then she couldn't speak as she was swept away on a final whirlwind of sensation that caused her to cry out in a stunning release of rapture.

She was vaguely aware that Roman was moving, accelerating, then she felt the convulsive shudder that shook him. He collapsed against her with a groan of total satiation. His broad chest was heaving and she could feel the trembling that shook his big body. "Roman." Her breath was coming in little gasps as she looked down at his head buried on her breast. "I don't understand. Why?"

"I don't understand either. But I don't think we'll play this fantasy again. I'll never be sure who is the slave. I feel enchained."

So did she. Bound and possessed and . . . uneasy. "I don't think there was any question who was dominating whom."

"No?" He moved off her. "That's because you couldn't see beyond the fantasy."

"I think I did see something else." She sat up and brushed a strand of hair from her face. "And I'm not sure I liked it."

"The fantasy?" He shrugged. "We'll find something else you like. I thought you were enjoying it."

"I was enjoying it. How could I help it? You're a fantastic lover. But you seduced me, and I don't like that one bit. I want to come to you freely and of my own will." She frowned. "And there was something else about you I didn't like—a darkness."

He smiled faintly. "I'm quite harmless and not at all kinky."

"I'm not so sure." She slid from the bed and began to gather her clothes from the floor. "You told me once you weren't a hard man, but that you often wished you could be." She straightened and looked him directly in the eye. "Well, I think you may be going to get your wish. I could feel the hardness in you tonight and I didn't like it."

"I thought you liked it very much. Put those clothes down and come back to bed and I'll try again."

"You know I didn't mean—" She drew a deep shaky breath. "I can't even talk to you. You've built a wall closing me out." She began to dress hurriedly. "Well, I've never been able to stand walls. If I can't break them down or go around them, then I usually set off and go somewhere else."

"No!" He was suddenly off the bed, standing, facing her. "I'm not going to let you leave me."

"I don't want to leave you." She could feel the tears stinging her eyes. "All I want to do is love you, but I can't stand this. Oh, hell!" She grabbed up her tennis shoes and ran from the bedroom.

"Manda, dammit, come back here."

"Not now." She was at the front door looking back to where he stood in the doorway separating the bedroom from the living room. "I refuse to let you tear me apart. Love isn't supposed to hurt like this."

"Is the great adventure turning sour? Love isn't always excitement and fields of pretty flowers. It can be pain and endurance and compromises. I'm not a knight in shining armor and you're not—" He stopped and then said wearily, "I don't know what you are, but I do know you're mine. In sickness and health, in light and in darkness."

The cynicism in his expression cut her to the quick. "I don't deserve this. Why are you . . ." She opened the door. "Good-bye, Roman."

"There's no use running away. I'll just come after you."

"No, don't come after me." The tears were running down her cheeks as she looked back at him. "I don't want to see you for a while. I can't afford to be this upset right now. I have work to do."

The door slammed shut behind her.

Roman stared at it blankly for a moment, before he slowly turned away. He felt as if his emotions had been first shredded and then burned. Tears. Manda. He had hurt Manda. Why did he feel so guilty? She had hurt him, too, and he was still hurting. Yet he couldn't stand the thought of Manda unhappy. And what if he were wrong? What if Manda were as bewildered as she seemed? What if she . . .

All these what-ifs were not solving the problem or doing him any good. The bottom line was that Manda may have betrayed him and it still made no difference in the way he felt about her. She was still warm-hearted, full of love and zest for living. Perhaps she didn't realize how he would view a breach of trust of this nature. He could be patient; he could subdue his own pain. He had known it wouldn't be easy when he had acknowledged to himself he loved

Manda Delaney, and yet he'd almost blown apart at the first challenge that love had presented to him.

He strode into the bathroom. He would shower, dress, and follow her. Lord knows, it might be only the first of many times when he would have to follow his quicksilver Manda. He might as well become accustomed to it.

The tears were running down Manda's cheeks and she tried to suppress her sobs as she ran toward the glow of the campfire in the distance.

Hard. He was so damn hard, ripping the fabric of the lovely dreams that had surrounded her. She didn't love him. She *wouldn't* love him any longer. As soon as she found the opal, she would go away and never see him again.

A blinding pain rocketed through her at the thought. Never see Roman again? Never see him smile or listen to his deep voice or have him touch her with desire and love? And there *had* been love tonight. A dark and tormented love, but love nevertheless. And pain. She had been conscious of Roman's pain even through the wall of cynicism he had built between them. Well, his pain was no business of hers. Why should she be the whipping boy for his moodiness? She suddenly stopped in her tracks. What was she thinking? If you loved someone, wasn't his pain your own? Oh, Lord, maybe Roman was right about her not knowing what love was all about. But if she didn't know about love, why did she hurt so much?

She could see Jacto lying on the tarp in the lean-to and hurriedly wiped the tears from her cheeks with the back of her hand. There was no use in letting

Jacto see how upset she was. Not that he wouldn't guess anyway. Jacto knew her too well for her to fool him for long. Perhaps she wouldn't have to worry about deceiving him. He was very still. He must be asleep.

She felt a tiny shiver of apprehension run down her spine. Something was wrong. Jacto was too still, and he never slept in the lean-to. He always liked to be where he could look up at the stars. "Jacto." She began running toward the lean-to, panic rising within her every second. "Jacto!"

Blood. A thin stream of blood was seeping through the blue and white bandanna Jacto had tied around his grizzled gray head. It was her own blue and white bandanna. Her knapsack was open and the contents rifled as if Jacto had been searching blindly for something to staunch the blood before he fell unconscious.

She dropped to her knees beside him, waves of sickness washing over her. "Oh, no, Jacto," she whispered. Had he fallen and hit his head or . . . What the hell difference did it make how it had happened? Jacto was hurt, maybe even dying. She had to *do* something.

She gently untied the bandanna from around his head. The flow of blood from the wound on the side of his head was very slow, not spurting. That was good, wasn't it? Or maybe it wasn't. She just didn't know. Her hands were shaking so badly she spilled half the water in the canteen before she managed to dampen the bandanna with the cold water it contained. She gently cleansed the blood from the wound. It wasn't as deep as she had feared, and the cold water was having the desired effect of staunching the flow of blood. Yet he was still unconscious and his breathing was shallow.

"Don't die, Jacto. *Please*, don't die. Just hold on, dammit." He probably had a concussion, but that didn't mean he was going to die. Lots of people lived with a concussion. She had to have help. He might need X-rays and blood transfusions and . . .

"I am sorry I took your bandanna, I could not reach my own knapsack." Jacto's voice was thin and reedy. "Naturally I will replace it."

Jacto's eyes were open! The wild surge of relief that spiraled through Manda made her dizzy. "Thank God. You're going to be all right. Lord, you scared me. What happened?" She frowned. "No, don't answer that. You probably shouldn't be talking. Close your eyes again."

Jacto's lips curved in a faint smile. "I do not wish to close my eyes. I am well now and in a little while I will be much better. There is no need for you to be frightened. I will not leave you yet."

Yet. Manda felt a pang of fear. She didn't want to think of him leaving her. She smiled shakily. "You'd better not. I don't know what I'd do without you."

His dark eyes were suddenly weary. "You will do what we all do. Go on. But not yet, not yet."

"Since you're going to be stubborn, you might as well tell me what happened. Did you fall?"

"No. I went back to the billabong and when I was coming back—" He shrugged and then flinched from the pain the movement caused. "Our intruder is back. I thought he had given up when he failed to return after that first night."

"Someone *struck* you? Did you see who it was?"

"No, he must have been waiting among the ghost gum trees. I heard a rustle and then I felt the pain."

He grimaced. "Much pain. I awoke later and came back here. It took great . . . effort."

"And then passed out again. You could have been killed. Why would anyone do that?"

"To remove me from the path," Jacto said simply. "I would have seen anyone who tried to go down into the shaft. The person who attacked me clearly wanted to see what you are doing down there."

"Violence. I never dreamed there might be any danger when I asked you to come with me. I feel so guilty." She ran her fingers distractedly through her hair. "Dammit, we may not even find anything. You could have lost your life over a heap of rubble and some bloody drawings of wombats and kangaroos."

"I thought the drawings were of birds."

"That was the other tunnel. This one has only marsupials," she said absently, her gaze still fixed worriedly on his face. "What difference does it make? I risked your life and—"

"You did not risk it. I guide my own life."

"Well, you can guide it right out of Deadman's Ridge. I'm not going to take the chance of having you hurt again."

"But you will stay." It was a statement, not a question.

"Beggars can't be choosers. Time's running out and this is the only shot I have at getting the money I need."

"But that is not all." His gaze was shrewd. "You still feel the opal is there."

She nodded. "You'd think I'd give up, wouldn't you? But I have the strongest feeling I'm right about the Black Flame being down there. Ever since I found the bird drawings, it's as if Charlie has been down there with me, helping me." She smiled. "I sound as if I'm the one who had the knock on the head."

"Perhaps your ancestor is guiding you. If so, you'd be very foolish to give up the search. We will stay."

"*I* will stay. *You* will go."

"I will think about what you say."

"Jacto, I'm not going to let you—"

"What the hell's going on here?" Roman's voice cut through her sentence. "Has there been an accident?" He was standing by the lean-to staring down at Jacto and the bloody bandanna in Manda's hands. "Why the devil didn't you come and get me, Manda?" He dropped to his knees beside Jacto. "What can I do?"

Manda experienced a sudden glow of warmth. Roman was here. She wasn't alone with her fear and guilt any longer. He would help Jacto. "Roman, it's terrible, Jacto has—"

"Had an accident," Jacto finished for her, his gaze fixed meaningfully on Manda's face. "But I am better now. I will sleep and wake and sleep again. Then I will be entirely well."

"I could get a doctor from Coober Pedy," Roman said. "Or we could take you to the clinic there."

"No." Jacto didn't look at him. "I am better off here."

"Jacto, perhaps having the doctor would be wise," Manda said gently. "Let Roman bring him here."

He smiled. "I have not lived all these years to let a doctor tell me how I am or what I am to do." He closed his eyes. "I guide my own life. I will sleep now. Go away."

"Jacto . . ." Manda gazed at him with helpless exasperation. His face was perfectly serene and his lids remained stubbornly closed. He had made up his mind and there would be no moving him. She sighed. "Okay, you obstinate old man, but you'd better get well soon. Do you hear me?"

His lids didn't open, but the corners of his lips curled in the faintest of smiles. "I hear you, Manda."

"Come on, Roman." She rose to her feet and stepped outside the lean-to. "Let him sleep."

"You're sure about the doctor?" Roman asked as he joined her by the fire. "He's an old man."

"No, I'm not sure," she said wearily. "I'm not sure about anything. Suddenly everything is falling apart around me. Why do bad things have to happen to people like Jacto? It doesn't make any sense."

"No." Roman's expression was very gentle. "I can't answer that, Manda. Bad things sometimes do happen and we just have to accept them and go on."

"That's what Jacto said." She gazed blindly into the heart of the flames. "He said someday he wouldn't be here for me and I would have to go on too. I'm not good at accepting things like this. I never realized it before, but I've always run away from unpleasant surroundings. I could always imagine something beautiful on the horizon, so I didn't see why I should linger where there was anything threatening or ugly. But I guess we can't do that forever. Oh, but I wish we could," she said, her voice and expression passionately wistful. "I wish we could see nothing but beauty and have kindness everywhere."

"I know you do." Roman was filled with empathy. Her nemesis was closing in and there was nothing he could do but stand by and wait and try to make the adjustment easier for her. "You're tired. You'd better get some sleep. I'll watch over Jacto." His lips twisted. "If he'll let me. I don't think he approves of me. He wouldn't even look at me when I was in the lean-to."

"That's right, he didn't. Strange." Manda rubbed the back of her neck to relieve the tension. "Maybe I will take a nap. Wake me—" She stopped. What was she thinking? There was danger here. What if the person who assaulted Jacto came back? She might not be able to persuade Jacto to leave, but she couldn't risk anything happening to Roman. "No, I'll watch over Jacto. He's my friend. You go back to your trailer."

"And you're my friend," Roman said quietly. "I won't leave you."

She felt a warm golden unfolding within her. Violence and sadness existed, but so did caring and beauty and love. Perhaps the balance wasn't so lopsided after all. She shook her head. "Please. I want you to leave. I'll be fine."

He frowned. "Look, Manda, I know you're upset, but we'll both have to forget what happened tonight at the trailer. Don't shut me out when you need me."

She looked at him in surprise. Since she had left him she had faced the possibility of death or serious injury to one she loved. In comparison, their disagreement now seemed trifling. He had come to her and given her support when she needed him, and that was all that was important. Yet if she were to send him away out of danger, it might be better if he wasn't aware of her change of attitude. He mustn't come here, and she would never feel safe in leaving Jacto alone to go to Roman. It would probably be best if he still believed there was an estrangement. She swiftly lowered her gaze to the fire. "It will be difficult to forget. I'm going to need some time. I don't think we should see each other for a while."

"That's bull," he said bluntly. "Do you think either one of us is going to undergo a miraculous change just because we're apart?"

"Maybe you won't, but I've been noticing some pretty big changes in myself lately." She tried to smile. "And I can't say I like it either; it's damnably uncomfortable. I need some time to myself."

His expression softened. "How much time? I'm not a patient man, Manda."

"You have a movie to shoot. Suppose we talk again when you're ready to wrap up the filming here and go back to Sydney."

He was silent for a long moment. "You do know that it's not going to be easy for either of us. I'm going to feel like marching down here and dragging you back to my bed at least ten times a day."

"And I'm going to feel like letting you," she whispered. "But I won't do it, because we need this time."

He was silent again. "I'll try. I won't make any promises, but I'll try." He hesitated. "Are you sure you won't let me stay and help with Jacto?"

"I'm sure. Don't worry about us. We'll be fine."

He smiled crookedly. "I'll worry. I've found it goes with the territory." He turned away. "Good night, Manda. If you need anything, for heaven's sake, come to me."

"Good night." She watched his retreating figure until it was a mere shadow in the distance. She was suddenly acutely conscious of how lonely and isolated it was here in contrast to the noise and bustle of the encampment to which Roman was returning. She experienced a wild desire to run after him.

She took an impulsive step forward and then

stopped. She couldn't run after Roman; she couldn't run anywhere. She had to stay and protect Jacto. He was her friend, and it was not only her duty but her privilege to care for him. The realization filled her first with surprise and then with an odd sense of serenity.

She turned, went to the lean-to, and crawled over to Jacto's knapsack. It took only a moment to locate his bone-handled hunting knife. Then she settled down beside him with the hunting knife in her hand and her gaze alertly searching the surrounding darkness.

Eight

"You have a call on the mobile phone." Dennis squatted down before their campfire and accepted the cup of tea Manda handed him. "I'm glad I caught you before you went down into that hole this morning." He made a face. "I don't know how you stand it down there. I'd get claustrophobia in no time at all. It's the wide open spaces for me. I guess that's why I became a pilot." He turned to Jacto. "How's the old bean? You look a lot more chipper than you did day before yesterday."

"I am well," Jacto said as he took a swallow of his tea. "The pills you brought helped to relieve my headache."

"Roman thought they would. He's been very concerned about both of you. I've had to report back to him every time I've strolled over here."

Manda felt a swift glowing warmth cut through the cloud of anxiety that had settled on her at the news of the phone call. It had to be trouble again. She hurriedly put down her own cup and rose to her feet. "Stay here and chat with Jacto, Dennis. I won't be long."

"Wait for me. I have to get back anyway." He finished his tea in two swallows.

"No, I'm . . ." She glanced at Jacto. It was broad daylight and she would be gone only a few minutes. He should be safe. "I'll be right back."

"I believe I will survive your absence," he said dryly. "I have managed for many years."

She made a face at him before turning and striding off briskly across the opal field.

Dennis fell into step with her. "You're worried about the old man," he observed. "I don't believe I've ever seen you worried about anything before. Is his head wound so serious?"

"No, a mild concussion perhaps. It scared me to death when it happened three days ago, but he's practically back to normal now."

"That's more than I can say for you." He gazed at her thoughtfully. "You look a bit frazzled around the edges. I don't mean to be overcurious about this mysterious business of yours, but is it really worth running yourself into the ground?"

"Yes."

"You know you can count on me to help, mate."

"I know." She smiled at him warmly. "Thanks, Dennis."

He grinned back. "As long as you don't make me go down into that hole with you, I'm at your service."

They had come to the communication shed, and Dennis gestured for her to enter. "I'll wait out here for you. It's hellfire hot in that shack." He leaned against the wall of the shed and reached for the cigarettes in his shirt pocket. "Then we'll walk over to the mess tent and have a bite of breakfast. The food's not half bad here."

She gave him an absent smile and disappeared into the radio shack. She came out five minutes later with a puzzled frown on her face. "Dennis, you like to place a bet now and then. Have you ever heard of a gambling casino called The Wombat in Brisbane?"

He shook his head. "Not that I remember. Is it important?"

"I think it could be."

"You know a lot of people. Isn't there someone you could ring? Government and media people usually have odd bits of information."

"No one in Brisbane." She brightened. "I know Jack Landford at the *Sydney Star.* I met him when he was in Christ Church on a story."

"Just the ticket. Give the man a ring."

She turned and walked back into the shed. This time she was gone more than a quarter of an hour, and when she returned, her frown was no longer puzzled but definitely worried.

"Trouble?" Dennis asked.

She nodded. "I have to get to Brisbane right away. I've just rung Addie and told her to meet me there. I hate to ask it of you, but will you take Jacto and me to Brisbane in the Cessna? I don't have much time. I think my sister may be sailing right into trouble."

"No problem. I have to drop some rushes off at the studio in Sydney anyway. I'll just make an extra stop in Brisbane. If you can be ready to leave Brisbane early tomorrow morning, I'll even pick you up on my way back."

"I'll try. I don't know how long this will take. I

shouldn't have to be gone long, if I can catch my sister before she leaves her apartment."

He grinned. "I've always fancied myself as one of those bloody knights rushing to the rescue of a fair damsel."

"Well, you'll definitely be doing that, Dennis. Thanks a million." She started across the opal field at a half trot, calling, "I'll fetch Jacto."

The feature article in the *Sydney Star* was spread over two pages instead of one this time, and the accompanying story included at least ten pictures and several amusing anecdotes of happenings on the set.

"I know what you're thinking," Dennis said quickly. "And you're wrong, Roman. Manda would never do this. She's too damn honest."

"You're being very protective." Roman didn't look up from the newspaper on the coffee table, and his voice was charged with tension. "And I'm wondering how you've suddenly become a mind reader." He paused. "Unless the same thought occurred to you."

"I've known you a long time and you were easy enough to read the last time this happened." Dennis's tone became persuasive. "Look, Roman, I flew Manda into Brisbane myself and then I picked her up there the next day. Brisbane, *not* Sydney."

"There are regular flights between Brisbane and Sydney, or she could have arranged to have been met and delivered the film in Brisbane."

"It was her sister, Sydney, who rang her. It was a family emergency."

"She appears to have an uncommon number of

convenient family emergencies," Roman said wearily. He felt sick. Just looking at these pictures made the bile rise in his throat. *Why*, for heaven's sake? He would have given her anything in the whole damn world. Why had she sold him out?

"You have fifty or sixty employees here in Deadman's Ridge. Any of them could have smuggled the story out."

"By carrier pigeon?" Roman asked ironically. "We've been watching the mailbag, remember?"

"There has to be some explanation," Dennis said desperately. "I know Manda. Whatever she's doing here has to be on the up and up. Confront her with this, Roman. Let her explain."

"I've asked her for explanations before. Hell, I've practically begged her to tell me why she's here. She won't do it."

"Then it all comes down to a question of trust, doesn't it? You'll just have to trust her, Roman."

A question of trust. How many times had Manda asked him to trust her? Trust me not to hurt you, she had said. Trust me not to betray you, trust me not to lie to you. How could he trust her? She was a child, a Peter Pan, a butterfly. Yet it had been no butterfly hovering next to Jacto the night he had been hurt. He could have sworn the child was at last becoming a woman. But the evidence was entirely against her and Dennis was right: It all came down to a question of trust.

He stared blindly at the pictures in the newspaper, lost in thought for many minutes.

Dennis watched him. "You're wild about her," he said softly. "Anyone with eyes can see that. Let me call in Security and have them investigate the rest of the crew. Give the girl a chance."

Roman became very still. His gaze narrowed on the article in front of him and something flickered for an instant on his face before it became shuttered. He carefully folded the newspaper and stood up. "I intend to give Manda a chance. Let's go see what she has to say."

"Right." Dennis sighed with relief. "You'll see, she'll have a good explanation." He turned to the door. "It's nearly sundown. She and Jacto should be having supper about now. We'll be able to catch her before she goes back down into the mine."

Roman nodded, his face still totally expressionless. "I just want to make a stop at the radio shack for a minute. I have a question or two to ask the communication operator and a call to make to Security in Sydney."

Manda looked up from the newspaper, her face pale, her eyes wide with disbelief. "You think *I* did this?"

"The pieces fit," Roman said impassively. "Every time you leave Deadman's Ridge the stories appear. You even placed a direct call to a reporter in Sydney before you left here the last time."

"She did that only to find out some information," Dennis protested. "I was right there."

"Or perhaps to set up a method to pass information," Roman said. "You appeared here the very first night I arrived in Deadman's Ridge and refused to explain what you were doing here."

Manda dazedly shook her head. He really believed she would betray him. "I had already been here for days before you showed up, and I couldn't tell you anything. Sydney, Addie, and I agreed not to reveal anything about our plans to anyone."

"How convenient. Your sisters also seem to be the reason for all your little trips."

The sarcasm in his voice flayed her raw emotions. Lord, she hadn't known she could hurt this much. "Yes, they were responsible. They needed my help and I gave it." Her hand clenched on the newspaper. "Roman, I would never do this. Don't you know me well enough to realize that?"

"The pieces fit," he said again.

"To *hell* with the pieces." Her eyes were suddenly blazing up at him. "Does everything have to fit in a neat little bundle for you? I would never suspect you of anything like this even if it were spelled out in black and white. Yet you're accusing me of being conniving, greedy, and completely unethical. For Pete's sake, I suppose you think I was the one who hit Jacto on the head too. What's a little assault to a monster like me?"

He went still. "Jacto was hit on the head? You led me to believe it was an accident."

"I didn't want to worry you. I was trying to protect you. Wasn't that stupid of me?"

"Dammit, you had no right to keep anything like that from me," he said harshly. "What kind of games are you playing here at Deadman's Ridge?"

"I can't tell—" She broke off. "It's no game, it's dead serious."

He smiled thinly. "*Dead* seems to be a rather prophetic word in this scenario. When you're dealing with violent assault, it opens entirely new horizons."

Manda wearily combed her fingers through her hair. "I didn't plan on telling you about that. It was a slip. You made me so upset. . . ."

Dennis gave a low whistle. "Lord, Manda, how could you keep something like that to yourself?"

"We're getting off the subject. The attack on Jacto has nothing to do with this." She slowly balled the newspaper in her hand, stretched her arm straight in front of her, and deliberately dropped the wad to the ground at Roman's feet. "I'm obviously not going to be able to convince you I wouldn't betray you. What do you intend to do about it? Have me thrown into jail?"

Roman was silent a moment, his expression once more guarded and closed. "I don't think that will be necessary. I could press charges for trespassing and possibly theft, but the newspaper story wouldn't be considered a criminal act. I feel the best course would be to send you and Jacto to a hotel in Coober Pedy tonight under heavy security to wait until I get a chance to investigate the matter further."

Manda's eyes widened in alarm. "And when will that be?"

"When I finish filming here at Deadman's Ridge." His lips curved in a crooked smile. "Wasn't that the time frame you gave me, Manda? Now you're the one who'll have to be patient."

"But I *can't* wait." Her voice was shaking with desperation. "You don't understand; that may be too late. I have to stay here and work."

"You're going to come with me right now." His tone was inflexible. "And I'm setting guards around the mine and your lean-to the minute I get back to the trailer to keep you or any possible cohorts you might have in my crew from trespassing again."

She took a step toward him. "Roman, please. I have the feeling I'm so close. Just give me a few more days here."

"Tonight." He started to turn away. "I'm fresh out of patience, Manda."

"No!" Her hand gripped his arm to prevent him from leaving. "All right, I'll tell you. It's the Black Flame, a forty-five-carat opal, and it's worth a fortune. It belonged to my great-grandfather, Charles, who hid it somewhere here in Deadman's Ridge before he was murdered over eighty years ago. I think he cached it in the mine."

"A very pretty fairy tale." He kept his face averted. "But you're very good at storytelling, aren't you?"

"Won't you believe anything I say? It's true, dammit. Charlie wrote his wife, Mignon, he had hidden the opal in a pouch within—" She broke off, her eyes widening in stunned surprise. "Oh, my Lord, that's *it*. Why didn't I realize it before!" Her face was suddenly radiant with excitement. "Roman, I *know* where it is. Just let me go down there right now and I'll show you."

"I'm tired of fairy tales, Manda." He still wasn't looking at her.

"Roman, dammit, I have to—" She stopped. It was no use. His expression was completely unmoved and more determined than she had ever seen it. If she didn't come willingly, he undoubtedly would force her. "I'll come with you. But I'll find a way of escaping from your blasted security guards. I'm coming back for my opal."

He didn't answer, but strode from the camp, obviously expecting her to trail meekly behind.

She did follow, very slowly and reluctantly, every nerve and muscle in her body on edge. So close. The frustration was going to drive her crazy until she could get back to the mine.

Dennis fell into step with her. "I'm sorry, Manda, I tried to help. He's a hard man to convince."

"He's a hard man, period," she said dully. She had become so excited, the agonizing pain she had experienced at Roman's distrust had been momentarily blunted. Now it was rushing back. "So hard."

"What are you going to do now? I don't believe for a minute you're going to cave in to him."

She shook her head. "I can't give up." She rubbed her aching temple. "And I can't wait for his lordship to get around to investigating my story. He told me there was a possibility he might be here for another two months. I'll just have to think of some way to evade his security people and get back here to the mine."

"Which will also be guarded," he reminded her. "It's a dicey situation."

"Will you help me, Dennis?"

He hesitated. "I have a damn good job, Manda. Roman will be mad as hell if I interfere."

"I wouldn't ask you if I weren't desperate. I didn't sell that story and any investigation will prove it. I just can't wait for an investigation."

He was silent for a moment. "Well, Roman is usually a pretty fair bloke. If you can prove your innocence, I don't think he'll hold my helping you against me." He smiled. "Okay, mate. What do you want me to do?"

"First, go back to the camp and find Jacto. As usual, he disappeared as soon as he saw Roman. Then contact Addie and Sydney and tell them I'm sending up a mayday. Jacto knows where to reach them." She smiled grimly. "Since it's partly their fault I'm in this mess, I think it's only fitting they help me bail my way out of it."

"Anything else?"

She tried to think. Her temples were throbbing with tension and she couldn't seem to think of anything but how flint-hard and emotionless Roman's face had been. Her gaze centered on him only a few yards ahead. His carriage was ramrod-straight and his spine as inflexible as his voice had been when he had confronted her earlier. Oh, Lord, she wished this aching would stop. She forced her fragmented thoughts into some sort of order. "I doubt if Roman's men will be keeping me in solitary confinement. When Addie and Sydney arrive in Coober Pedy, bring them to me at the hotel and I'll try to have some sort of plan ready."

"I'll do better than that. I'll pick them both up in Sydney and fly them in myself."

"Oh, would you, Dennis? That would be wonderful." A frown knitted her brow. "And would you ask Brent Penrose to come too? He might be willing to help."

Dennis grinned. "You remind me of a general marshaling her forces. Are you going to launch a guerrilla attack on Deadman's Ridge?"

"You're joking, but it might come to that." Her smile was mirthless. "I wouldn't be at all surprised if it did. Caesar's commanding general may just have to create a submissive fantasy from his own point of view."

"Caesar's general?" Dennis asked.

"Never mind," she said wearily. She wished she hadn't thought of those last wild moments in Roman's arms. It brought a montage of memories tumbling back and caused the pain to increase tenfold. "It's not important."

She would strive with all her might to make that statement true. She couldn't afford anything Roman had done to be important to her right now. She had to block out both the hurt and the love she felt for him. Oh, God, why couldn't she stop loving him?

Block it out. Forget the pain. Remember only the Black Flame shimmering, glowing, waiting for her in the darkness of Charlie's mine on Deadman's Ridge.

Nine

Brent Penrose's expression was wary as Manda opened the door of the hotel room. "I'm here. I certainly don't know why I'm here. I have an idea I may have lost my mind."

"Come in." Manda stepped aside to permit him to enter. "I'm very grateful to you for coming. Dennis just rang from the airport and he and my sisters should be here any minute."

"That's nice. I always did like family reunions." He looked around the small shabby room. "Not exactly the Ritz, is it? I would have thought Roman would be more generous."

"The Ritz? You've got to be kidding. Roman would have liked nothing better than to throw me into the Bastille."

"So I've heard." He shook his head. "You should have realized that selling those pictures would send his temper soaring."

"I didn't sell those pictures. I didn't have anything to do with it." She closed the door and leaned wearily against it. "I just can't prove it right now. Do you believe me?"

He studied her thoughtfully before he nodded slowly. "Yep, I think I do." He suddenly grinned. "I can tell you're a lady of impeccable taste, and you would *never* have given that picture of a cannibal camel top billing over me."

"Never," she agreed, smiling back at him. "So will you help me?"

His expression became cautious. "I didn't say that. Those two security men I passed in the hall look like doubles for Arnold Schwarzenegger. They could do serious and permanent damage to my profile."

"Well, then everyone would have to take your acting seriously, wouldn't they? You might even get a few gangster roles. Maybe even a remake of *Public Enemy* or *Key Largo*."

"Somehow I don't think that was the way I wanted to break out of the mold." His lips twisted. "Though if Roman finds out I visited you in your room, I may not have a choice. I've noticed he's very possessive of you. Since you became his lady, I haven't even been able to mention your name without getting a glance that would turn a uranium core into a block of ice."

"I'm not his lady. Not any longer."

"Aren't you?" His gaze was skeptical. "Then why are you stashed here instead of in Sydney being prosecuted? My guess is that Roman's keeping you close until he has a chance to get over his first anger. Then I'll bet he'll be showing up here to try to work things out. Yes, I think you're definitely still his lady."

"I don't know." She shrugged. "Everything's changed. It was so perfect and now—"

"Roman never pretends to be perfect. It's one of

the things I admire about him. He just works like hell to make whatever he's creating perfect."

"Well, I'm not perfect either, but I would never have accused him of—" She broke off. "Oh, what's the use? I didn't ask you to come here to solve my romantic problems. I need your help to find a way of getting back to the mine."

He instantly shook his head. "There are two security men at your camp who make the guys in the hall look like Woody Allen and Don Knotts."

A smile tugged at her lips. "Do you always think in movie terms?"

"I guess so. It's the world I live in."

"And you love it?"

"Sometimes. Sometimes I hate it." His smile was lopsided. "I'm an excitement junkie. My work is exciting and I'm hooked on it. Fame can be a kick too. Yeah, I guess the highs come more often than the lows."

"Excitement," Manda repeated. "I think I might be able to fill your cup to the brim. Want to give me a chance?" Her amber eyes were suddenly glowing and her voice became a soft velvet persuasion. "Think of it, Brent. A real-life adventure that will equal anything you've ever done on the screen. A search for a lost treasure, the charge of the light brigade, danger."

Brent was gazing bemusedly at her face. "Get thee behind me, Satan. Dennis once mentioned you could be a Lorelei."

"There's nothing satanic about this. We're the good guys. Strictly white-hat stuff." She grinned. "I wouldn't want to ruin your image."

"Why do I feel I'm being seduced by the Force? I don't know—" He was interrupted by a knock on the door and gave a mock sigh of relief. "Saved!"

"Not necessarily. That will be Sydney and Addie." She turned to open the door. "And if you think I'm a siren"—her eyes were twinkling as she glanced back over her shoulder—" 'you ain't seen nothing yet, buster.' "

And when Manda introduced her sisters, he fully understood what she meant. *Siren* was the operative word for the women who stood facing him. They were both dressed in casual slacks and blouses, but there was still a subtle, almost romantic allure about them. And they were both absolutely stunning. No, he decided, it was Sydney who was stunning with her long dark wine-colored hair and clear golden eyes. Addie's appeal was gentler, like the caressing mist of a mountain waterfall. It was strange she should have that effect, Brent thought. Addie's short red hair and enormous dark eyes should have been more striking than soothing.

He smiled. "I'm very happy to meet you both. Would either of you like to go to bed with a movie star?"

They both looked at him in surprise.

Manda chuckled. "Don't pay any attention to Brent. I think he extends that offer to every woman he meets."

Brent looked hurt. "You malign me. I'm usually very particular. It's only when I've been placed in a position of forced celibacy that I lose my innate shyness." He gave a slight bow. "But I guarantee any and all of the Delaney sisters will have a standing invitation, no matter what the future competition."

"Thank you." Addie's face lit with a roguish grin. "We appreciate your condescension."

Sydney nodded. "Do you suppose he'd even give us his autograph the morning after?"

"Ouch!" Brent's expression was pained. "I suspect

you ladies are capable of being less than appreciative of my charm."

"However, we'll be most appreciative of your help,"
Manda said as she turned back to her sisters.
"Where's Dennis?"

"He went back to Deadman's Ridge to fetch Jacto,"
Addie said as she sank down in the sun-faded beige
wing chair by the window. "Jacto insisted on staying
near the mine last night to make sure no one stole
any of your possessions."

"Is there such a thing as room service at this
hotel?" Sydney wiped her brow with an immaculate
linen handkerchief. "I have to have something to
drink. How can you stand it here, Manda? There's
so much dust everywhere. I don't know how Dennis
even managed to land."

"The dust storms sometimes rise to fifteen thousand feet." Manda smiled sympathetically. "And,
sorry, no room service. These aren't exactly the kind
of exotic surroundings you've been accustomed to
lately, are they? I guess I've gotten used to it."

"I could go out and get something," Brent offered.

Sydney gave him a radiant smile that made him a
little dizzy. "Would you? I'm terribly thirsty."

It had been a long time since he'd been used as an
errand boy, but Brent imagined that smile could
send any man fetching and carrying. "I'll go right
away."

"Wait," Manda said. "Are you going to help us,
Brent?"

"I'm thinking about it. I've almost finished my role
in the picture and Roman would lose a hell of a lot of
money if he decided to cut my throat now. Your
version of The Charge of the Light Brigade sounds
interesting." There was a fugitive gleam of excite-

ment in his deep blue eyes. "It reminds me of that old western classic, *The Magnificent Seven*, only we'd be the Sensational Six. What do you want me to do?"

"I'm going to need a big diversion while I slip down to the mine. You're permitted to go anywhere on the set and the location. Could you possibly get hold of some special effects items, something that would cause a lot of smoke and explosions?"

"Probably." He looked disappointed. "That's not exactly a cavalry charge."

"Oh, we'll have that too," Manda assured him, trying to smother a smile. There was something endearingly boyish about Brent. "Straight through the encampment."

"Hot damn." Brent's face brightened. "Do you want me to steal the horses from the corral?"

Manda hesitated. "Well, we're not going to use horses. I thought borrowing the four camels would be more effective. Everyone seems to hate them so much and—"

"The Sensational Six has just dropped to the Fabulous Five." He glowered fiercely at her. "Do you think I'm crazy? Those camels stay awake all night trying to think of different ways of plotting my doom. *No camels!*"

"It will be perfectly safe. I'm putting Addie in charge of the camels."

"You have something against your sister? Even if she did steal your dolls when you were in rompers, you shouldn't try to get your revenge this way. It's too gory to contemplate."

"Please believe me, Mr. Penrose." Addie's soft voice dropped into the conversation like a ripple in a crystal pool. "I know animals. I make my living as a blacksmith. I won't let them hurt you."

"You're a blacksmith?" He shook his head in disbelief. She was slight, fragile, and as dreamy-eyed as one of his groupies. "You've got to be pulling my leg."

She shook her head. "I'm a very good blacksmith." She smiled gently. "You can trust me. I'm sure we can make Manda's plan work."

"No, I'm—" He broke off. He found to his astonishment that he did trust her, even to the point of risking his nose to that man-eating, knock-kneed carnivore. "I'll have to think about it."

Manda smiled. He would do it. Addie had worked her usual magic and even Brent Penrose had no talisman to withstand her particular sorcery. "You do that. I figured you and Addie would come charging into the encampment from the north and Jacto and Dennis would come in from the south."

"Where do I fit in?" Sydney asked.

"I need someone to lure the security men away from the mine."

"The Fabulous Five just became the Fantastic Four," Sydney said flatly. "Why me? I couldn't lure a horse dying of thirst to water. I wouldn't know how to go about it."

Brent started to laugh and then stopped. She wasn't kidding. She actually didn't realize a woman with her beauty was a magnet and had no need for wiles. "I don't think you have to worry."

Manda nodded. "Maybe you could pretend to be drowning in the billabong. You'll think of something. I have the greatest faith in you."

Sydney frowned. "Dammit, Manda, why do I always get the hard jobs?"

"I'd be glad to trade you the camel," Brent offered politely. "Though I doubt if my allure would be quite as effective with those security men. Of course, I could try batting my ravishingly long lashes at them. But those beefy macho types are notorious for their violent defensiveness about their masculinity, and I might end up being tossed in the billabong."

Sydney laughed. "We wouldn't want that to happen. I guess you'll just have to stick to the camel."

Brent sighed. "I knew it was too good to be true." He turned to leave. "I'll go shopping at the local supermarket and pick up some refreshments."

The door closed behind him.

Sydney's gaze immediately zeroed in on Manda's face. "You look ten pounds thinner, thoroughly exhausted, and something else." She frowned. "Something . . . different."

Manda slowly shook her head. "Stop mothering me, Sydney. I'm fine, or I will be as soon as this is over and I have the opal in my hands."

"You really think you know where it is?" Addie asked.

"Yes." Manda crossed the room to the window seat, sat down on its print cushion, and leaned her head back against the wall of the alcove. "I really do." She gazed out through the sheer nylon drapes to the street below. Coober Pedy. Dust, near-intolerable heat, and men and women so dazzled by the lure of opals they were willing to live underground to escape their surroundings. She would be glad to leave this town and the desolate country in which it stood. It had taken too much from her and given nothing back but heartache and disillusionment.

Yet would she leave the same Manda who had

come here only a few weeks ago? She had the notion that a new Manda might have been born here.

The sun was going down now and the shabby room was assuming the kindly golden veil of twilight. It was very peaceful sitting here with Sydney and Addie in silent companionship. None of them felt the need to break the tranquility of the moment. They seldom needed words.

It was a long time before Sydney said quietly, "You're not happy."

Manda's gaze remained on the street below. "I'll get over it. How are things with you?"

"I saw the black swans fly."

Manda turned to look at her. The simple sentence meant so much more than the words expressed, and it was all there in Sydney's face. "I'm so glad for you." She looked at Addie, sitting in the wing chair. "Unicorns?"

Addie's smile was serene as she nodded. "Unicorns."

Manda leaned her head back against the wall again and closed her eyes. They were both finding what they had sought on that childhood odyssey so long ago, and she was happy for them. She just wished she had been as lucky. For a moment she felt terribly lonely and isolated, but then Sydney reached out and clasped her hand and it was all right again.

She opened her eyes and smiled mistily at them. "Hey, didn't I tell you we had only to hold on and we'd get to our island eventually? You both gave up too soon the last time."

"And are you giving up too soon now?" Addie's dark gaze was probing.

Manda's eyes widened in surprise. "I don't . . . know," she said slowly. Was she letting bitterness and hurt rob her of what she wanted most in the world? Was she running away again? "I believe I'd better think about it."

"It would be a good idea." Sydney's smile was teasing. "Most people do spend a *little* time on self-examination, Manda."

Manda returned her smile. "Then I'd better get in the swing of things, hadn't I?" Her hand tightened on Sydney's and she included Addie in the intimacy of her smile. "Help me?"

Neither of her sisters answered. There was no need for them to reply. Manda knew they would always be there to give her what she needed. They were a team, the Delaneys of Killaroo. No matter where they wandered, a strong tie would still exist between them.

The golden-limned shadows deepened in the room and they were silent once again—remembering, thinking, storing quantities of peace, love, and togetherness to carry them through the challenge to come.

"She bit me on the *ass.*" Brent's tone was as outraged as his expression.

"Shhh. Do you want to wake everyone in the whole encampment?" Manda was trying desperately to stifle her laughter at Brent's astonishment and indignation. "We have to get these camels out of the corral before the trainer—"

"But she bit me on the *ass.* I just turned my back for a second and she—" He turned to glare accusingly at Addie, who was busy saddling the fourth camel. "You promised you'd protect me."

"I'll have a talk with her as soon as I'm finished here," Addie said soothingly. "She's probably upset only because she's surrounded by all these strangers."

"Strangers?" Brent repeated, incensed. "I'm certainly no stranger to her. She's become very familiar with every portion of my anatomy. Bite by bite."

"That's because you're so sweet, mate." Dennis mounted his kneeling camel. "You notice my tough hide hasn't come under attack."

"He probably thinks you're a camel too," Brent said sourly. "You show the same insensitivity." He edged closer to the animal in front of him. "Look at her, she's grinning at me. She's just waiting for me to get on her back so she can run off to the desert, where she'll have me at her mercy."

Manda leaned against the wooden post of the corral, her shoulders shaking helplessly with laughter. Her carefully planned guerrilla attack was rapidly becoming a farce. "Please," she gasped out. "We have to get going. It will be light soon and we need every advantage we can get. Addie, for heaven's sake, do something about his animal so we can get out of here."

Addie walked over to Brent's kneeling camel, placed her hand squarely between its protruding brown eyes, and began stroking gently. "She'll be fine. She really likes you, Brent. Camels can be very complex." The camel's eyes became soft and dreamy as she nudged her nose affectionately against Addie's breasts.

"Well, I'll be damned," Brent said blankly. "I think you've hypnotized her. Make her stay like that for a minute." He rushed forward and got into the saddle. "Now tell her I'm a true son of the desert and she's not to bite me or try to knock me off or—"

"Come on, Brent." Dennis's voice was suddenly impatient. "Let's get this show on the road."

"*I've* already gotten it started. I planted the smoke bombs and the explosives last night"—Brent checked his watch—"and they're scheduled to go off in exactly six minutes. That's more than you've done, Dennis."

"I got rid of the security men at the hotel," Dennis said belligerently. "I'd like to see how you would have done that little job."

"How *did* you do it, Dennis?" Manda asked. "I was really worried about how we would manage to slip by them."

Dennis glanced down to check his reins. "I put a mickey in the coffee the delivery boy brought over from the shop across the street. Then I pulled the sleeping beauties into the linen closet."

Addie gave Brent's camel a final pat. "I don't think she'll give you any more trouble. Stay close to me, though."

"Don't worry," Brent said grimly. "There's no way I'm going to let her get me alone."

"Are you okay, Jacto?" Addie asked as she turned to mount her own camel.

Jacto nodded as he touched his camel and it obediently lumbered to its feet. "We understand each other."

Manda turned away. "Sydney should have had time to draw the security men away from the mine by now. I'll be on my way. Six minutes."

"Good luck, Manda," Addie said quietly.

Manda lifted her hand in acknowledgment and hurried away.

She would need all the good luck she could get, she thought, worried. Timing was everything even with the confusion and distraction provided by the smoke and the camel charge. Whatever ruse Sydney used to get the guards away from the mine couldn't be counted on to keep them away long; Roman would realize almost at once what was happening and storm down to the mine. At most, she had calculated she had ten minutes to find the opal after the assault began. Once it was found, she didn't care if she was discovered or not. If necessary, she would be able to give it to Addie and Sydney to take to a dealer while she waited out Roman's blasted investigation.

It was almost light and her steps quickened. Her campsite appeared to be deserted, so it followed that Sydney must have been successful. She crossed the last few yards at a run, grabbed the lantern from the lean-to, and lit it hurriedly. She snatched her tool kit and started to turn away. Then she stopped, impulsively turned back, set the tool kit down, and rifled through her knapsack until she found her silver and turquoise medallion. It couldn't hurt, she thought as she slipped the necklace over her head. This particular piece of jewelry had always been symbolic of Delaney luck and had once belonged to Mignon.

She picked up the tool kit again and ran for the opening of the shaft. The first explosion went off! Her gaze flew across the opal field; huge puffs of white smoke were billowing into the air. Another explosion sounded and a sudden flare of orange lit the gray morning sky at the opposite end of the encampment.

Manda grinned as she began to negotiate the metal steps leading down into the mine. Brent had obviously done his work well, and with his customary dash and sense for the dramatic.

The ladder seemed longer than usual and the talcum-fine dust instantly assaulted her lungs as she reached the bottom of the shaft. She carefully picked her way around the rubble, the glow of the lantern forming strange, alien shadows on the rough walls. When she had first started her search, the narrowness of the tunnels had made her feel smothered, almost claustrophobic, but now she scarcely noticed it. Charlie's mine was as familiar to her as her bedroom at Killaroo. She moved quickly from the primary area to the offshoot tunnel she had been searching for the last week.

She felt a sudden surge of panic. What if she were wrong? No, she couldn't be wrong, she reassured herself immediately. In his letter Charlie *must* have been trying to give Mignon a clue to where he had hidden the opal. He had probably been afraid something might happen to him and his letter might fall into the wrong hands, so he hadn't dared give her more than a hint. A pouch within a pouch. But the second pouch wasn't the protective one Manda had first assumed. At least, she desperately hoped that it wasn't.

She lifted the lantern high and examined the paintings on the rough black-brown rock walls of the tunnel. Which one? A wombat, a possum, a kangaroo. They all had pouches.

"Which one, Charlie? I don't have much time," she murmured.

The large black eyes of the painted animals stared blindly at her from the wall. Waiting.

The kangaroo, she decided with strange surety. She moved quickly toward the last figure painted on the wall of the tunnel.

The kangaroo was standing upright, her slender forepaws appearing fragile and helpless compared to her massive hindquarters. Charlie had captured both the strength and the appeal of the marsupial with clever strokes of his paintbrush. The painting itself was merely an outline in black, as were all the other paintings in the cave. The natural brown color of the walls themselves filled in the outlines and Charlie had only had to add shading here and there to suggest fur or muscle or . . .

Shading. There was shading around the pouch area of the kangaroo.

Manda's hands were shaking as she put the lantern and her tool kit on the ground and took a step closer to the painting on the wall. "Oh, Charlie, please!"

The tips of her fingers carefully traced the wide band of dark shading outlining the kangaroo pouch. Porous. A filler of some sort that had been painted over. She quickly opened her small tool kit and extracted a file. The point of the file sunk into the porous filler like a hot knife into butter. She turned the file and a powdery dust began drifting from the shading. She held the file with both hands and began to move the tool carefully, following the shaded outline of the pouch. In a few minutes she had completely encircled the outline of the pouch area and she dropped the file to the ground.

She took a deep, quivering breath. Then her hands reached forward slowly, her fingers slipping into the narrow opening she had made on each side of the pouch. She pulled gently. It didn't move. She pulled a little harder. The stone that comprised the kangaroo's pouch pulled out of the wall! She drew the stone all the way out, set it on the ground, and peered into the dark cavity.

It was there! A large leather pouch!

Her heart was beating so hard she thought it would leap out of her breast as she carefully took the pouch from its hiding place. "Charlie, you'd better not have been a practical joker."

The Black Flame glowed in the lantern light like a rainbow at midnight. It was a large square stone, uncut, unpolished, but totally magnificent. Semi-transparent, it shimmered with veins of green, blue, and scarlet like the burning heart of the flame for which it was named.

Manda stared at the opal, mesmerized by the sheer beauty of the jewel. What must Charlie have felt when he had uncovered this natural wonder? Joy, fear, a sense of reverence that such beauty should exist even in the darkness and corruption of Deadman's Ridge? Perhaps all of those emotions.

There was a piece of notepaper within the pouch, but she didn't want to read it now. It was probably a note to Mignon and she felt she had intruded enough in Charlie's world today. "It's for Killaroo, Charlie," she whispered. "Your dreams were never fulfilled, but this will help another Delaney find his dream. I think you would have liked that." She carefully slid the opal back into its pouch and drew the strings tight.

"I'll take that."

She jumped. Then she realized to whom the voice belonged, and relaxed. "Lord, you scared me, Dennis. Don't worry about the opal." She turned toward the shadowy figure standing at the entrance of the tunnel. "I'll just put it into the tool kit and it will be perfectly sa—"

He was holding a gun!

"Dennis?"

He took another step toward her, the gun held almost casually in his hand. "Congratulations. I should have known you'd get what you were after. You always were a determined little sheila."

Manda shook her head in bewilderment. "What are you doing, Dennis? You're my friend. You're no thief."

"There are times when you have to weigh friendship against other values."

"Money?"

"In a manner of speaking. My Cessna is on the line. I got in over my head on the ponies and a few other games of chance and put the Cessna up for security. I can't lose the Cessna, Manda. You know how I love that plane, how I love flying."

"I know." Her hand tightened on the pouch. "Don't do this, Dennis. It's not worth it."

"It's the only thing I can do," he said simply. "It's just a matter of time until Roman finds out I sold the pictures and set you up. Then I'll lose my job with him and probably be blackballed. I've got to have a stake to pay off my debts and start somewhere else. The money I received from the pictures wasn't a tenth of what I owe." His gaze went to the leather pouch in her hand. "But that opal might be just the ticket I need to set up shop somewhere else."

"It's *mine*, Dennis. I've worked myself into the ground to find Charlie's opal."

He nodded regretfully. "I'm sorry about that. You know, I think I half hoped you'd never find what you were looking for. I didn't want to have to take it away from you. I like you, mate."

"Yet you're pointing a gun at me."

"Necessity." His lips twisted. "You love that old Abo. I knew you wouldn't be complacent about giving me the opal when you found out it was me who gave him the tap on the head."

"You!"

"You hadn't figured that out yet? I needed money and you were obviously looking for something valuable. I thought I'd take a peep and see what you were up to."

Manda felt sick. "You could have killed him."

"Be reasonable, Manda, I couldn't lose my Cessna."

She gazed at him in disbelief. "A human life balanced against an airplane?"

He gestured impatiently with the gun. "The opal. I don't have much time. I slipped away as soon as the smoke bombs started going off, but there's bound to be someone hotfooting down here soon."

"What will you do if I refuse?"

"Don't," he said softly. "I'm a desperate man. I might just have to shoot you. Oh, not to kill. Just an arm wound or—" He broke off, the words gurgling in his throat. He swayed and then buckled forward to the ground.

Manda dazedly stared at his still, slumped figure. What had happened?

"Are you all right?" Roman asked.

Her gaze flew to the taller shadow that had replaced Dennis's at the end of the tunnel.

Roman stepped around Dennis's inert body and strode toward her into the lantern light. "God, I felt sure you were going to jump him any minute. Why the hell didn't you give him the bloody opal? I would have gotten it back before he'd reached the steps to the surface."

"I didn't know that," she said numbly. "What did you do to him?"

"A well-placed karate chop to the back of the neck.

A little something I picked up in 'Nam." He stopped in front of her. "I was afraid to wait any longer. You weren't about to give up the opal and he had that damned gun."

"How long did you wait? What are you doing here anyway?"

"I've been here since a little before three o'clock this morning. The security men at the hotel called me and told me you were having a meeting resembling the staff meeting before D-Day. I wanted to be here when Dennis made his move."

"You *knew* it was Dennis?"

"I knew he was probably the one who had sold the pictures and the stories. When I called Security in Sydney, I told them to find out the extent of his debts and try to nose around the newspaper and gather more evidence. I didn't want him to fly the coop, so I decided to let him think I still suspected you." He shook his head. "Then you sprang the assault on Jacto on me and I suspected Dennis was also the one behind that. Hell, I didn't know what the devil to do. I didn't want you or Jacto in danger, so I had to move you to Coober Pedy." His lips twisted wearily. "Then Jacto flitted away again and I knew damn well you wouldn't stay at the hotel for very long either. I was prepared for you to launch a full land and air attack to get back here, and from the sound of the explosions on the surface, that's exactly what you did do. Do I have anything left up there to finish my picture?"

She nodded. "It was only a harmless diversion. How did you know he sold the stories?"

"Once you were eliminated, he was the logical choice. He moved freely between here and Sydney and there were a few anecdotes in the last story that took place on the set. You were working night and day here at the mine and wouldn't have had access to the stories."

"Someone on the production crew could have told them to me."

"Yes." He smiled slowly, tenderly. "But I decided trust had to start somewhere. As Dennis said, it's all a question of trust."

She felt a wild soaring of joy rising within her. She wanted to leap into his arms and hug him with all her might. She wanted to sing and shout and dance. "He was wrong. It isn't all a question of trust, but it's sure a hell of a lot. We'll go into the rest later." She took a step nearer and touched his cheek gently with the tips of her fingers. "But not here. This is Charlie's kingdom and I've taken enough from him today. Let's go up to the real world." She grinned. "And I'll tell you why it was so important that I find the Black Flame, and I'll introduce you to my sisters."

Ten

"Hot damn!" Brent gave a low whistle of appreciation as his gaze traveled over her. "Manda, the magnificent. I didn't think you owned any clothing but
shorts and cut-off jeans." He was only half serious.
He had received a distinct and very pleasant shock
when Manda had stepped from the plane. The outfit
she was wearing was elegant, sexy, and still totally
Manda. The emerald green material was the softest
chamois imaginable, and it molded her body, issu-
ing an irresistible tactile invitation. The top was
merely a sleeveless vest with a few buttons left fash-
ionably undone to reveal a lush bounty of cleavage.
The A-line skirt was slit to the thigh and, as she
walked toward him, he could see tempting glimpses
of long, tanned legs and beautifully arched feet shod
in high-heeled Grecian sandals of Moroccan leather
which criss-crossed and tied at mid-calf. "I'm impressed."

She made a face at him. "It wasn't you I was
trying to impress. Where's Roman?"

"He had to direct one of the last action scenes of the picture. I wasn't in it, so he asked me to meet you here at Coober Pedy." His lips curved in a lopsided smile. "It surprised the hell out of me. Knowing Roman, I would have expected him at least to insist on providing you with a bodyguard before he let me within ten feet of you."

Manda smiled serenely. "Haven't you heard? Roman's into trust these days."

"Maybe," Brent said skeptically as he helped her into the Jeep. "But I think I'd better disappear before he sees you in that outfit." His gaze skimmed lightly over the soft brushed chamois molding her full breasts. "He'd never believe I resisted temptation in my present celibate state." He got into the driver's seat and turned on the ignition. "Even *I* don't believe it. How did your business in Sydney go? Did you sell the opal?"

She shook her head. "The jeweler is trying to locate a collector who will give me a better price. He told me he'd call me later today with a final bid." She moistened her lips. "It's going to be close. The jeweler offered me only three hundred and fifty thousand for the Black Flame. I've got to get more than that."

"You will." Brent backed and turned the Jeep. "Any lady who could persuade me to hop on a camel is capable of any feat of magic."

Manda laughed and settled back on the seat in preparation for the long trip to Deadman's Ridge. She could feel the eagerness and anticipation rising within her as each mile passed. She hadn't seen Roman in four long days, and, though she had spoken to him on the phone every day, it hadn't been enough. She had left with her sisters on the afternoon she had found the Black Flame. She'd discovered in Sydney that locating a buyer for a rare opal was far more complicated than she had thought possible.

By the time she had boarded her flight this morning, she had been nearly crazy with impatience. She had been wildly disappointed when she had seen Brent, instead of Roman, waiting for her when she had arrived in Coober Pedy. It was foolish, perhaps, but she had wanted Roman to see her in something more feminine than the rough clothes she had been wearing since the first night they had met in Deadman's Ridge. Who was she kidding? She had dressed carefully, fully conscious that she was being frankly seductive. She smiled as she remembered she had once indignantly accused Roman of seducing her. Now the tables were turned. It had been far too long since they had come together in love, and she meant to remedy that as soon as possible.

It was late afternoon when the Jeep began its uphill climb to Deadman's Ridge.

"Do you want me to drive you to the location where they're shooting the scene?" Brent asked.

She shook her head. "I'd just be in the way. Drop me off at the perimeter of the opal field. I'll walk down and let Jacto know that I'm back."

"I told him I was going to the airport to pick you up. He said to tell you he'd wait to see you."

"*Wait* to see me," she repeated, puzzled. "That's a strange way to put it." She suddenly felt a tiny frisson of fear.

She jumped out of the Jeep as soon as it stopped and started hurriedly across the opal field. By the time she reached the lean-to, she was almost running. Jacto's knapsack was missing from beneath the tarpaulin!

He was gone. But he *couldn't* be gone. Jacto wouldn't leave her. "Jacto, dammit, where are you?"

"I am here."

She whirled in the direction of the billabong and let out a low cry of relief. Jacto was coming toward her, flowing from the ghost gum trees with his usual wiry grace.

"Jacto, you scared me. I couldn't find your knapsack and—" She stopped. His knapsack was fastened on his back. "You're leaving?"

"It is time."

"But you'll be coming back? You always come back."

He didn't answer.

"You *have* to come back. We're a team, remember? No one in the world understands—" Her voice kept breaking and she tried to steady it. "Why?"

"You have changed. I have not."

"But that doesn't make any difference. I'm still Manda. I still care about you. I still need you."

"You walk a different path now." For an instant there was a flicker of pain in his expression. "It is a path I have never been able to travel. All my life I have watched it happening. For a day or a year or a decade I have someone to walk with me and then the change comes and I must go on alone."

"Jacto . . ." Her throat was so tight she could scarcely speak. "Stay. You'll like Roman, if you give him half a chance. I know you have some prejudice against him but—"

"I have no prejudice. He will make you a fine husband. He knows you well."

She frowned. "But you refused to meet him, even to look at him."

"It is painful to look at the bearer of sorrow. I knew he was the one who was to lead you to the new path."

Manda felt the tears brim and then roll slowly down her cheeks. "Please . . . stay."

He shook his head. "It is time." He turned away and started across the opal field.

Her fists clenched at her sides. The sobs were welling in her throat, but she refused to release them. Tears wouldn't convince Jacto to stay or to return. Nothing would convince him. Except perhaps . . .

She took a step forward and her voice rang out over the silent emptiness of Deadman's Ridge. "Jacto, dammit, you come back to us. If you won't come back because of me, then there's another reason."

He continued to walk away from her. He did not look back.

"Do you know the kind of children Roman and I will have? Think about it. They're bound to be as wild and free and crazy as we were. They'll want to run the rapids and climb the Blue Mountains and walk the same paths as we did. They'll need someone to walk those paths with them." She stopped for breath and tried to steady her voice. "Do you hear me? You come back, Jacto."

He stopped and stood very still for a long moment. Then he glanced over his shoulder and the corners of his lips deepened in a faint smile. "I hear you, Manda." He turned away. "I will think about what you have said."

Nothing else. She watched helplessly as he once more started across the opal field toward the distant winding road.

He did not look back again.

• • •

Roman parked his Jeep beside Manda's and climbed out of the driver's seat. At first, he didn't see her, then he caught a glimpse of jewellike emerald and a glint of silken gold against the dark gray of the ancient cleaved rock. Manda was standing in the exact spot where the rock was shorn in two, her gaze on the desert spread out before her. In her elegant outfit she should have appeared totally out of place in these primitive, desolate surroundings, but somehow she didn't. She looked wild and basic and . . . beautiful.

He climbed the slight incline and walked toward her, his gaze searching her face. "I've missed you." That was the understatement of the year. He had felt miserably incomplete while she had been gone. He had an idea it would always be like that now. "I wanted to meet you at the airport, but it was important I finish shooting that scene. I have to try to wrap up the filming here before it's time to go to Melbourne and watch Addie's bid for the Cup."

"I knew you'd have been there if it was possible. I've missed you too," she whispered. Her gaze returned to the limitless stretch of land before her. "The brook is gone; so are the flowers."

"Yes, I told you they wouldn't last."

"You told me they would come back though."

"They will come back. I promise you, Manda."

"Jacto is gone too."

"I know. Brent told me he had left when he gave me your message to meet you here."

"I'll miss him."

He took a step nearer and gently touched the shining wing of hair sweeping back from her temple. "I can't promise you he'll come back, Manda."

"I know you can't." Her lips were trembling as she smiled at him. "He guides his own life. I hope you don't mind, but I've promised him our firstborn child. Perhaps all our other children too. I thought it would be a lure he couldn't resist. Our kids will probably need all the help they can get. Who knows? They may want to set out to find a mystical island where unicorns live and black swans fly and there are adventures every single day and—" Her voice broke. "I think they could find that island with Jacto."

He felt his throat tighten helplessly. How he wanted to help her, but all he could do was share her sorrow, not banish it. "I think so too." His arms enfolded her carefully, and he rocked her tenderly. Poor little Peter Pan, face-to-face with her nemesis at last. No, it wasn't Manda who was Peter Pan, but Jacto. Manda had come to terms with maturity as Roman himself had done eight years before, and in her own individual way. She was no tame Wendy, but his wild, bright-plumed Manda, whose warm, loving heart was aching now. His lips brushed her temple. "Maybe someday we'll go there too. I can't promise you adventures every day, but I'll do my damnedest to make you happy, love."

She lifted her lips and kissed him. "But I *will* have adventures every day. I'll be growing and changing and learning to love you more and more." She smiled. "If it's possible to love you more. You were wrong, Roman, when you said I didn't know what love was all about that day we were here. I may love you more now, but I did love you that morning. I just needed a little time to think about what it meant." She looked him directly in the eye. "And for your information, even when I thought you were being a suspicious bastard, I decided you were worth sticking around and reeducating. I do want to share dreams and make those dreams come true. I think I can handle the sickness-and-health clause, too, but there's not going to be any darkness in our life, Roman. We're going to be so happy that we're going to light up the whole bloody world."

He laughed. "You bet we are." She was bouncing back. The sadness was still there, but he could practically see the joyous indomitable vitality that was the essence of Manda returning with every passing moment. "We'll show them all what a marriage should be."

"The first thing I'll have to do is perform some first-class surgery." One finger touched the scar on his left cheek and traced it down to the corner of his mouth. "You need a few hangups removed and I'm just the lady to wield the scalpel. Let's get one thing straight, you're *not* ugly."

He frowned. "Manda, I—"

Her fingers swiftly covered his lips. "Be quiet and let the surgeon have her say. You're not handsome, but you could never be ugly. You have too much intelligence and character in your face to ever be unattractive." She grinned. "And you're the sexiest man on the continent of Australia and maybe even the whole world. I can't be in the same room with you without wanting to rip off your clothes and— What are you doing?"

"What does it look like I'm doing? I'm undressing you." His swift fingers finished unfastening the last button on her chamois vest. "You should never say things like that to a sex-starved man without expecting an instant reaction." He parted the vest and inhaled sharply. "I didn't think you were wearing anything underneath it. That chamois clung like a second skin."

His head bent and she felt his warm breath searing her nipple. Her fingers tangled in the thick crispness of his dark hair. She was suddenly breathless. She could feel the fluid heat between her thighs and her muscles were clenching with familiar tension. "We're going to make love . . . here?"

"I think it's entirely appropriate, don't you?"

She wasn't sure she could think at the moment. "The rocks . . ."

"I'll get a blanket from the Jeep." He looked up and smiled. It was a beautiful smile. "That's a lovely outfit, but I'd like to see you wearing only the sunlight and the desert, Manda, and I want to remember you belonging to me in this special place." He wanted something more; he wanted to erase the last traces of sadness clinging to her and replace them with a memory of joy.

He drew her gently to the ground and was suddenly looking down at her with dancing eyes, his face illuminated by laughter. "Don't you want to make love with the sexiest man on the entire continent of Australia?"

Tenderness, love, and laughter were gazing at her from Roman's face. How could she answer anything but what she did?

"Oh, yes." Her arms slid up his shoulders and around his neck. "By all means, love, I could hardly let an opportunity like this pass!"

The sun had gone down, but there were still a few delicate streaks of pink in the deep indigo of the sky as they walked back to where the Jeeps were parked.

"It's so beautiful." Manda stopped and looked out over the panorama of earth and sky. "It makes me feel small, yet . . . powerful. It's as if I'm a part of it all, an extension of all that strength." She shrugged. "Do you know what I mean?"

He nodded. "I know." He gazed out at the horizon. "I have something to tell you. The jeweler from Sydney called before I left the encampment. He was able to get a firm offer of only four hundred thousand for the opal."

Manda experienced a sinking disappointment. "Damn, I was afraid of that."

"I suppose you won't take the last hundred thousand from me?"

"Not if I can think of any other way." Her brow wrinkled in a frown. "There has to be something I can do."

"There is." Roman smiled. "I've already done it. I didn't think you'd accept money from me, so I made a few phone calls."

"Phone calls? To whom?"

"One magazine in Sydney. Then two overseas calls to *People* magazine and *Rolling Stone* in the U.S."

"Magazines?"

He nodded. "We're about to have the most publicized wedding since Prince Andrew married Sarah. And for that publicity you're going to receive a great deal of money, my love. One hundred thousand dollars to be exact."

She was gazing at him in bewilderment. "But you *hate* publicity."

"But I *love* Manda Delaney."

Oh, and she loved him. What a beautiful thing to do! She threw herself into his arms and hugged him with all her strength. "Roman, you're wonderful, you're fantastic, you're—"

He chuckled. "I like the sexiest man in Australia superlative best. That definitely bears repeating."

"The sexiest man in Australia, in the Pacific, in the universe!"

"That's enough." He kissed her with loving sweetness. Then he made a sound low in his throat, drew her closer, and kissed her again, roughly, and with searing passion. He lifted his head and said thickly, "I was wrong. It's not enough. It's never enough. Let's go back to the trailer and go to bed."

She laughed up at him. "It's not even dark yet."

"It will be soon, and if we're not in bed by the time it is dark, I guarantee I'll be seeing what you look like wearing starlight." He gave her a quick kiss and turned her firmly in the direction of the Jeeps.

His arm encircled her waist as they walked. "Now, I've been thinking about the tax question on the five hundred thousand dollars. That's going to be a tremendous bite, but I think I've come up with a solution."

She nestled contentedly closer. "You have?"

His expression was thoughtful. "Suppose you sell me the story for a screenplay? It has possibilities. Three sisters, a near-impossible quest, danger, love. There's no reason why you . . ."

And Manda's joyous laughter rang out in the timeless stillness of the outback night.

Epilogue

Hell's Bluff, Arizona

"Did you see this story in *People* magazine?" Sierra Delaney glanced at Deuce playing solitaire at the card table across the library. " 'The wedding of the year.' How can anyone stand to have their private lives spread all over the tabloids like this?"

"Not everyone has a privacy fetish like the Delaney clan." Deuce skillfully plucked a jack from the middle of the deck and placed it on the queen of hearts. "The news of your marriage to York didn't break in the media until almost two months later."

"But these are Delaneys too. Australian Delaneys, that's what caught my attention. The bride is a Manda Delaney and her two bridesmaids are her sisters Sydney and Addie Delaney. According to this story, they appear to be . . . extraordinary. I guess it's not possible they're distant relatives?"

"It's a common enough name." Deuce played a seven of diamonds on an eight of clubs. "And, as far as York knows, the Shamrock Trinity are the last of the line. Though there have been a few bogus relatives who have cropped up from time to time to try to acquire a bit of the Delaney lucre." He smiled with satisfaction. "Ah, I've won again."

"Of course you won. You always win. You even cheat at solitaire. I can't see how you can possibly regard the game as any kind of challenge."

"But I won *faster* this time," Deuce protested indignantly. "I cut my previous time by a full minute and a half. You have no appreciation of the intricacies involved in high-speed cheating at solitaire." His lips thinned. "And I wouldn't be reduced to solitaire if you or York would give me a decent game now and then."

"Neither of us have masochistic tendencies." Sierra tossed the magazine aside. "You've been sticking awfully close to the house lately. Could it be you can't get a game from anyone else in Hell's Bluff?"

"Let's just say it's become a tad more difficult." Deuce gathered up the cards and started to shuffle, his graceful fingers moving with artful delicacy. "This town is beginning to cramp my style a bit."

Sierra's smile faded. "And is York beginning to feel cramped too? In the last few weeks I've noticed something . . . different. He's getting restless again, isn't he?"

"A little perhaps. He's been busy winding up his business in Hell's Bluff for the last year in preparation for going home to Killara. This is a big step for him. You can't expect a renegade like York to adjust to the idea of permanence in the flicker of an eye. I think he needs to get away from here for a month or two before he settles down." He looked up from his manipulation of the deck to smile faintly. "Don't worry, he's not going to wander off into the sunset and leave you. York's more in love with you now than when he married you twelve months ago. If he does take off, he'll definitely take you with him. He can't do without you."

"And I can't do without him," Sierra said softly. "Which means I don't like to think of him even a bit unhappy if there's any way I can prevent it. Why the devil didn't he tell me he wanted to get away for a while? He knows I'd follow him to the moon."

"He also knows you've been very happy here," Deuce reminded her. "He told me once he intended to give you everything you ever wanted. He's aware that a home and a place in life are high on your list of priorities, and he realizes how close you've grown to his brothers and their wives. He doesn't want to tear up any roots you may have planted." Deuce's one brown eye regarded her soberly. "He'll never make a move to disturb those roots, Sierra. You'll have to do it for him, and he may give you a hell of an argument."

She nodded. York would fight tooth and nail if he thought she was sacrificing herself for him. "I'll think of something." She glanced at the clock on the mantel. "York should be back soon from taking Kath to the heliport. I'd better go upstairs and change. He said he was taking me to Melanie's place to celebrate with a meal par excellence. Are you going with us?"

"You must be joking. The opportunity to indulge in the first meal in thirteen months that won't give me indigestion? How can I resist?"

Fifteen minutes later, Sierra had changed into a red and white flowered dress of paper-thin voile that floated around her like a summery cloud. She ran a brush through her short dark hair and started downstairs. As usual, her gaze went straight to the portrait of York's ancestress, Rising Star, on the wall of the landing. She had grown so accustomed to the portrait in the last year, she now looked on the Apache woman almost as a living being.

"We have a slight problem, Rising Star," she murmured as she paused on the landing. "He's going to be very difficult about this unless I manage to handle it just right. Sometimes these Delaney men simply don't know what's good for them."

She had started down the stairs again, when the front door opened and York walked into the foyer.

"You're dressed." He took the steps two at a time until he reached the step on which she was standing. "And very elegantly too." He dropped a kiss on the tip of her nose. "I won't be long. I only need to shave and change my shirt." He rubbed his jaw back and forth against her cheek. "You feel good. I never get used to how soft and silky you are. Want to come up and help me dress?"

"We'd never get to Melanie's." Her arms went around him and she buried her cheek against his chest. Lord, she was lucky to have him love her. Strong, passionate, and tender, he was everything she had ever dreamed a husband could be. "Do you realize we've never taken a honeymoon?"

His fingers tangled in her hair and he pulled her head back to look into her eyes. "You told me you didn't want to go away on a honeymoon." He kissed the hollow of her throat lingeringly. "You were right. It would have been a complete waste. As I remember, neither of us would have made it out of the bedroom to do any sight-seeing."

"But we're an old married couple now. Maybe we

should take a long trip before we settle down at Killara. It may be our last chance for a long time."

His sapphire-blue eyes narrowed on her face. "Why this sudden urge to roam?"

She carefully avoided his gaze. "I just thought it would be nice to—" She broke off. She'd better back away and attack from a different angle later. She had never been able to lie worth a damn, and York knew her too well not to see through any excuse she might fabricate. "Never mind, we'll talk about it later." She kissed him lightly on the lips. "Go get dressed. I'm starved."

He slowly released her. "Sierra . . ."

She was already going down the stairs and glanced back over her shoulder. "You know, I'll really miss Kath. Do you think Rafe will keep her at the ranch for long?"

"I have no idea. He didn't set any time limits when he called and asked me to send her to Shamrock." He frowned. "I have an idea my little brother is trying to pull a fast one. He was entirely too self-sacrificing about taking her off our hands for a while. I would have suspected something at the time, but all I could think about was storing away my antacid pills for a few months." He turned and started up the stairs. "I'll be down in ten minutes."

Sierra watched him climb the steps, a tiny frown knitting her brow. She had to think of a reasonable explanation to give York for her sudden desire to leave Arizona. The delayed-honeymoon suggestion had certainly sunk like a lead balloon.

The phone on the table in the curve of the stair-well suddenly rang, abruptly jarring her out of her pensiveness. She crossed the few yards to the table and picked up the receiver.

"Oh, hi, Maggie, we were just talking about you and Rafe. Did Kath make it? Good." She listened for a moment. "The Delaneys of Killaroo? I've just read the story in *People*, but Deuce said . . ."

The conversation continued for another five minutes, and when Sierra hung up the receiver, a delighted smile curved her lips.

"Well, you look pleased with yourself." Deuce was standing in the doorway of the library. "Rather like the proverbial cat who devoured the catnip as well as the cream."

"Do I?" Sierra's dark eyes were dancing. "I believe I've found you new worlds to conquer, Deuce. Can you imagine an entire country populated with people who have never heard of the infamous Deuce Moran?"

"Are you planning on unleashing our Deuce on an unsuspecting society?" York drawled as he came down the stairs. "What's all the excitement about, Sierra? You're glowing like a diamond-wreathed Christmas tree."

"I've just talked to Maggie at Shamrock and she told me the most amazing story." Sierra turned away from the phone and looked up at York, standing on the landing. "About a lovable rogue named William Delaney, a sheep station called Killaroo, and three sisters who made a pact." She smiled coaxingly at him. "How would you like to take Deuce and me on a little jaunt to Australia?"

HANDSOME, SPACE-SAVER
BOOKRACK

LOVESWEPT

Love Stories you'll never forget by authors you'll always remember

BANTAM
SHOP-AT-HOME
C·A·T·A·L·O·G

Special Offer
Buy a Bantam Book
for only 50¢.

Now you can have Bantam's catalog filled with hundreds of titles plus take advantage of our unique and exciting bonus book offer. A special offer which gives you the opportunity to purchase a Bantam book for only 50¢. Here's how!

By ordering any five books at the regular price per order, you can also choose any other single book listed (up to a $4.95 value) for just 50¢. Some restrictions do apply, but for further details why not send for Bantam's catalog of titles today!

Just send us your name and address and we will send you a catalog!